I0690991

The Field of Mustard Seeds

Songs of the Willow Tree, Volume 1

Lakise Collins

Published by Lakise Long-Collins, 2022.

While every precaution has been taken in the preparation of this book, the publisher assumes no responsibility for errors or omissions, or for damages resulting from the use of the information contained herein.

THE FIELD OF MUSTARD SEEDS

First edition. August 19, 2022.

Copyright © 2022 Lakise Collins.

ISBN: 979-8218061036

Written by Lakise Collins.

Chapter One

I can't stand to take another breath...it hurts. The pain is too much for me to handle. A broken heart is all I have known. Every night I go to sleep and hope that I won't wake up in the morning. But to my dismay, my hopes are in vain. If God truly exists, he must surely hate me to let me go on in this way. So I must take matters into my own hands... I'm sorry, Grandpa. Goodbye.

Willow looked down with weary eyes like puddles toward the paper filled with words that left her empty inside. The note had seemed like a good idea at first, but no matter how hard she tried, she just couldn't quite capture her feelings and put them on the page. Willow impugned her whole approach, because in her mind it all meant nothing. She realized that it didn't really matter if she left them an explanation. No one would care once she was gone; maybe they would even be happy to not have to worry about her anymore. With discontent and aggravation, she aggressively balled the letter up, as the puddles could no long hold themselves together and gently ran down her face in streams. "I can't do this anymore!" she roared at the top of her lungs, throwing the note to the floor. Willow quickly grabbed it back up, staring at it with dissatisfaction. She violently ripped the note bit by bit and tossed it in the air. Then she fell to the ground and rolled up into the fetal position as the pieces swiftly scattered throughout the grim room.

A GIANT SHADOW SLITHERED into the room, joining the others that were swarming around Willow, being ever so careful not to give any visual awareness of their presence. The others acknowledged him when he entered and stood at attention.

"It's about time he got here," one solider whispered to another.

"Grrrrr... WHAT did you say, you filthy *NINCOMPOOP*?" the chief snarled with rage at the solider.

"Ss—s—sorry, sir," the small solider mumbled to his chief.

"You don't have any authority here. I do, and I get here when I please. You got a problem with that? You're a sorry excuse for a demon!" He got in the minion's face with gritted teeth.

"N...no sir." The solider trembled.

"Anyone else got a problem with that?!" He raised up and addressed the rest of the group.

"No sir!" they all yelled at once.

Another messenger came and gave a report to the aggravated leader. "She finally gave up her key to you know who yesterday. She renounced it during an argument she had with her grandfather. When she woke up this morning her energy was very low; we made sure to keep the atmosphere heavy in here. I think she is really going to do it this time."

"Hmmm.... Splendid.... Hahaha...." The chief's rambunctious laughter exploded in the air as the room grew darker with the echo of his voice.

AS WILLOW CONTINUED to cry in a ball on the floor, she recalled what her grandpa had always told her, "The Lord will never put more on ya than you can bear, honey." Willow quickly grabbed another sheet of paper off of her computer desk and scribbled the words "It was too much for me." The words rang profusely in her mind over and over again as she picked up the bottle of pills that sat on the desk beside her.

Earlier she had sneaked into her mother's medicine cabinet and found a bottle of Hydrocodone left over from her knee surgery. She figured that they would be strong enough to get the job done.

Willow looked over at her alarm clock, which read 11:00 AM. *Good. No one should come home for a couple hours,* she thought to herself, because her mom didn't get off work until three in the afternoon and her brother was in school. She opened the bottle of pills and poured them out into her cupped hand. There were only 10 pills left. "This should do the trick, but just in case," she muttered while grabbing another bottle. This time she opted for the sleeping pills that she had been taking for the past week because her racing mind no longer allowed her to go to sleep at night. The bottle was sitting on the computer desk next to a large bottle of Grey Goose Vodka that she had been guzzling all morning.

Willow took a deep breath and filled her mouth with the handful of Hydrocodone, washing it down with a big gulp of vodka. She coughed, overwhelmed by the number of pills and strength of the drink, forcing her to tightly cover her mouth with her hand, making sure everything went down her throat. Immediately after, she took another giant swig of vodka.

It didn't take long for the drugs to kick in. Minutes later she felt lightheaded and dizzy. It was getting harder and harder for her to open her eyes after each blink. Suddenly her legs gave out, and it seemed as though an invisible force pushed her down, causing her to fall to the floor. Fighting tired eyes that wanted to sleep, she glanced across her room until her eyes froze on the necklace that hung over the jewelry box on her dresser.

"WILLOW, COME DOWNSTAIRS, I want to talk to you sweetie," David yelled. He rubbed his hand over his head, combing through his short curly black hair. His other hand rested on his slender waist as he pondered how he was going to give the heartbreaking news to his little girl.

A few minutes later, David heard small footsteps skipping down the stairs. Willow turned the corner to enter the kitchen, tightly holding her favorite baby doll. David was sitting on one of the stools by the island in the middle of the room. "Yes, Daddy?" she answered with a welcoming grin. When David saw her, his hazel eyes lit up and dimples appeared through his wide smile. "Come, baby girl," he beckoned, stretching out his arms with open hands towards her. She ran as fast as her little feet could, without tripping over her long pajama pants. She jumped up onto her father's lap and he gave her a big hug.

While in her father's arms Willow could smell his cologne. It was a smooth scent, not too strong. She loved it because it made her feel safe and comforted.

"I have something to tell you and I know that you won't like it." Willow just listened with a blank look on her face.

"Daddy has to go away for a while..."

"No, not again," Willow whined, interrupting her father.

"Yes, yes, I have to go, I must and you know we have already talked about how important my duties are for the safety of this country, right?" David said with a stern voice.

Willow's head hung low. "Right," she whispered.

"I am scheduled to go back to Iraq."

"But you just came from there!" Willow shouted, lifting her head back up to declare her argument.

"I know, sweet heart, but this is how the army is and I am committed to it. I am not only protecting the country, but I am also protecting you in the grand scheme of things. It is important for you to know that once you start something and commit yourself to it, you must stick it through and complete it."

"I know," Willow said in a frustrated tone. She dropped her head once more, defeated. She didn't really understand the tragedy that had taken place in New York City, or the thing called terrorism that was frequently talked about since then, but all she knew was that she hated it for taking her father away once again.

David lifted her chin gently. "I know you don't like that I'm not around much anymore, and neither do I. But just trust me, sweet heart, that will change very soon. Until then, I have something for you. It's a gift for you to keep while I am away. With this, a piece of me is with you always, and before you know it I will be back." With a pleasant smile he reached into his pocket, and then placed a balled-up fist in the air. Willow playfully tried to peek through his fingers.

"What is it, Daddy?" Willow asked with piqued curiosity. Swiftly opening his hand, a silver necklace dangled from his fingers with a big circular medallion locket at the end. It was intricately decorated, with sparkling rubies embedded around the edge. She unhooked the necklace from around his index finger and held it in her hand. "Wow, this is beautiful," Willow whispered, staring in amazement. She had never owned anything so valuable.

"Look, it gets better." David grabbed the medallion and in the center, his favorite scripture was engraved in small print. He read aloud....

"Blessed is the man that trusteth in the Lord, and whose hope the Lord is.
"For he shall be as a tree planted by the waters, and that spreadeth out
her roots
by the river, and shall not see heat cometh, but her leaf shall be green;
and shall not be careful in the year of drought, neither shall cease from
yielding fruit.
Jeremiah 17:7-8"

Willow listened to the words elegantly flowing out of her father's mouth. Her eyes were wide with excitement as she examined the necklace closer. The rubies, which were her favorite part because they were her birth stone, glistened in the light of the bright morning sun that trickled into the kitchen through the open blinds. This created a kaleidoscope effect of oranges, blues, purples, and greens melting inside the true red of the stones.

He handed her the necklace so Willow could explore her gift even more. She opened the locket up, and inside was a silly picture of her and her parents making funny faces, which was taken in a photo both during their vacation at Disneyland the week before. She let out a little giggle, looking up at her father. "Now, take a look on the back," he said eagerly.

She turned it over to the back and read aloud. "To my heart."

"Oh, I love it, Daddy! Thank you!" She hugged him tightly with joy in her heart, which made tears well up in David's eyes.

"I wanted to go ahead and give you your present, because I won't be here for your ninth birthday on Saturday. I must leave tomorrow morning," he whispered. All of a sudden there was a pain in her stomach and her heart dropped. She had been so overwhelmed with the gift that she had almost forgotten that he had to go away again. But reality came flooding back, and for some reason extreme fear came over her.

She looked up at him. "Please don't go this time, Daddy; I don't have a good feeling about it."

"Don't worry, sweet heart, everything will be ok; remember, I will be back before you know it," he said with a tear falling down his cheek.

"Well, promise me you will be back by Christmas," she pleaded.

"Now Willow, you know I can't promise you that; I am not sure when I will be back. We have talked about this plenty of times."

"Yes," she answered shortly.

"Look, I know you may not understand now, but no matter what happens, know that I love you and God will protect me while I'm away. He will protect you and mommy also. Okay?" She nodded her head. He and her grandpa often talked to her about God, and they all went to church on Sundays. They often read scriptures, much like what was engraved on her locket, but she really didn't understand the concept of

God. It was hard for her because she couldn't see him, or even touch him. Even though she didn't understand, she would often talk to this mysterious being that she was told loved her. So hearing her dad say those words somehow eased the pain.

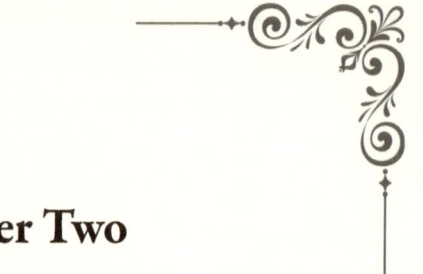

Chapter Two

Willow opened her eyes, slowly blinking from the bright morning light that peeked through her window blinds. She wiped her eyes, and then did an enormous stretch that tossed the sheets off of her and onto the floor. She felt the coolness of the chain around her neck. It startled her at first, but then she grabbed the necklace and smiled, finding comfort from the gift her father had given her. Suddenly, she sat up as though she had remembered something of high importance.

Jumping out of bed, she ran out of her room and down the hallway into her parent's room. It was empty; no one in sight. She yelled "Daddy" over and over again, looking under the covers of their bed, then running to the bathroom, then back to the hallway, to no avail. He was nowhere to be found. "You up, honey?" her mom called from downstairs. Willow urgently ran down the stairs and into the kitchen to find her mom making breakfast. Out of breath she gasped,

"Where's Daddy"?

"Oh, sweetie, he left early this morning around 4:30. He didn't want to wake you because you were sleeping so peacefully."

Disappointed, Willow plopped in a chair at the table. Her mother continued on.

"He told me how upset you were when he told you he was leaving; don't worry sweetheart, he is going to be just fine. Your daddy is a strong man and a great hero; you should be proud."

A wave of grief came over Willow and the fear returned with vengeance. She screamed "No, he can't go," and she ran straight out the front door, still screaming at the top of her lungs. Tammie ran outside after her, trembling from her daughter's hysteria. She had never seen Willow overreact like this. Tammie grabbed Willow by the arm, stopping her, once she caught up with her at the end of the driveway. Willow yanked her arm out of her mother's grip, fighting to get away while screaming even louder, "Daddy come back, please come back!"

"Baby it is gonna be ok! It's ok!" Tammie put a stronger grip on her daughter. Willow began to calm down from exhaustion. She surrendered to her mother's hold and pleading voice. Defeat infiltrated her heart and she dropped her face in her hands, falling to her knees.

Tammie looked down worriedly at her sobbing daughter, who was collapsed at her feet. She had been so caught up with her own pain due to her husband's absence that she didn't notice the devastating effect it was having on her baby. Kneeling down, she tightly wrapped her arms around her daughter. She stroked Willow's curly hair, humming a melodic tune. After a long moment of peace, Willow looked into her mother's eyes and said very calmly, "He won't be back, Momma." A chill when down Tammie's back as she reflected on the words that had just came from her child's mouth. They stayed there in that same spot embracing each other in silence for close to an hour.

Weary in spirit, Willow was haunted by the memory of her father as her breathing grew long and shallow and her limbs felt like bricks. She was unable to clear her blurry vision, because her eyes were begging for rest. Then a slight movement in a dark corner of the room caught her attention and a burst of adrenaline opened her eyes wide to investigate. Lurking in the corner, a dark silhouette appeared, and due to her fuzzy vision she was unable to make out what it was. Giving up on their mission, her eyes could no long remain open, and the figure leaped out in her direction, just as her eyes closed for the last time.

WILLOW OPENED HER EYES wide and popped up horrified, vigorously kicking her legs. She finally stopped and looked around, still thinking of the creature she had seen coming towards her from the corner of her room. To her surprise, she was no longer in her room and the creature was nowhere to be found. She was relieved to find that she was alone. *But where was she,* she pondered, as she pushed herself up from a graveled trail. She began to brush dirt off of her clothes and slowly did a 360, taking in the scenery. This place was like none she had ever seen. It was like a magical land, something made up in fairy tales. Everything was perfectly placed, like it was cut from a magazine.

The first observation that took her by surprise was the trees. They were all gigantic, with vast branches stretching in all directions and big leaves of a vivid apple green color. But the best part of it all was the fruit that sprung forth, the biggest apples and peaches she had ever seen, so plump, so juicy. She repeatedly wiped her eyes to make sure they were telling her the truth. Entangled down the trunk were vibrant vines decorated with colorful, round objects. They reminded her of the candy she loved, Skittles. As she got closer she realized they were berries that glowed like lit ornaments on a Christmas tree.

Walking up closer to one of the trees, she examined it from top to bottom. She didn't miss one detail of the spectacular sight. The top of the towering tree seemed to extend all the way into the glorious sky, and a glorious sky it was. The gentleness of the fluffy periwinkle blue sky reminded her of how she had spent hours and hours gazing up into the heavens as a little girl. The vastness of the horizon was like a canvas of an intriguing painting with clouds of cotton balls, showing off a hint of pink swirls in them. "Wow!" she gasped, watching in amazement as the birds glided across the painting without a care.

She rubbed the back of her neck; a cramp had formed from staring up into the distance for far too long. Looking across the span of the land, she was captivated by the bushes and the grassy plains with rolling hills in the distance. They wore the same apple green as the leaves of the trees, but the bushes had some darker shades intertwined within. This gave them great depth and dimension, making them stand out even more. The bushes yielded a different type of fruit, which were the shape of bananas while having the color and texture of strawberries. Perplexed by the odd fruit, she was tempted to taste one, but she was too afraid that they could be poisonous.

Walking along, she admired the grass, because it was furnished with all kinds of beautiful flowers. "Where am I?" she asked herself as she spotted a bunny rabbit scurrying through a cluster of lemon drop daisies. "This can't be real; I must be dreaming," she said as she continued down the path to further explore the vivid wonderland.

FAR OFF IN THE DISTANCE, he evaluated her every move, peering at her from the comfort of his cave. "She's here and the time has come...." he said as he turned to the others.

WILLOW FOUND SOMETHING new around every turn as she ventured deeper and deeper into the forest. Straight ahead she got a glare from something shiny; it was water. Drawing closer she saw that it was a gorgeous river with crystal clear water. She reached the riverbank, which was covered with a bed of lime green moss, and she leaned forward to get a better look. The water sparkled like little diamonds were floating on the surface reflecting the sunlight. It was so clear she could see straight down to the sandy riverbed.

The deep water was filled with fish of all different shapes and sizes peacefully swimming downstream. Scattered along the river's floor laid red pebbles that reminded her of the rubies on her medallion. Her eyes followed along the side of the riverbank. About three miles down there was a point where the river divided into four separate streams. Unable to see from where she stood, she wondered to what other mysterious lands they all journeyed.

Even though she was enchanted with curiosity exploring the uncharted territory, she began to question whether her attempt to take her own life had been successful. Maybe she was just going out of her mind, hallucinating this elaborate adventure from the drugs she had taken. *But that couldn't be, because everything seemed so real, even right down to the sweet aroma in the crisp clean air,* she thought as she took in a deep breath.

A rustling sound in the bushes interrupted her thoughts and frightened her. She swiftly turned around to face the unknown in the shrubs. Searching all around, there was no one, but she felt as if she were being watched. Her voice cracked with fear. "Who's there?" No one answered, just the sound of leaves dancing within a gust of wind.

As she turned back around she caught something peeking from behind a tree nearby out the corner of her eye. Jumping back around she shouted, "Who's there? Come out and show yourself!" Then all in one swift motion, it came out of its hiding place. Willow was taken aback by the image before her eyes. During her exploration of the land she saw animals she had never known existed, but none of them compared to this creature.

It had skin that was a rich, shimmering copper gold, which looked smooth to the touch. Its body frame was the build of a man with a fuzzy sheet of indigo hair. It also wore indigo hair framing around its face, like a lion's mane. The ears were shaped like the bell end of a trumpet horn, which were slightly peeking through its mane. The face was of a man as well, but its nose was a small snout protruding over its mouth. The eyes were big and round, matching the indigo in its hair, with swirls of icy blue.

Even though the creature was strange, Willow was memorized by the beauty it displayed. Each feature was immaculately formed and placed just right. The eyes gripped her as if it saw straight to her core, leaving her frozen speechless with shock. "Hello Willow," he said taking a giant step towards her. His voice was very raspy and had a deep undertone, so she was sure that it was male. The strangest thing was, when he spoke it was as if he were singing. Whole chords of harmony lived in each syllable he spoke, like a grand piano was being played. The notes he uttered she was sure were not on any scale known to man.

She stared in silence for what seemed like forever, while her mind raced in panic. It took everything in her to keep her composure, but she grew more and more anxious. *Should I run? But where will I go? Am I going crazy? Is he going to eat me...? Wait, did he just say my name?* All sorts of things ran through her head as she continued to panic. Finally, she came to a conclusion. *I'm gonna run for it,* she thought. As if he had read her mind he took a step back, raising his sharp hairy claws, and said "Wait.... I do not wish to bring you harm, I am here to show you the way, child." The more he spoke the more Willow wanted to hear, as if she were being seduced.

The melodies that flowed from his mouth relaxed her. Regaining her natural breathing pattern, she asked, "Who are you and how do you know my name?"

"My apologies for not properly revealing myself. My name is Dregus keeper of the garden. At your service," he said as he bowed with his eyes fixed on her.

"And how do you know me?"

"I know all about you Willow. I have watched you for a very long time."

"You've watched me? What - who are you?

"Let's not dwell on futile things, child, soon you shall know all there is to know."

"Well, at least tell me where I am," she demanded in frustration.

Dregus slowly walked up close to her, exposing his long lanky tail, which was gliding on the ground with his every move. The closer he got to her the more she became aware of how tall he was. Towering over her, he bent down so his face met hers and said, "You are back where it all began....... Eden," with glowing eyes and his mouth curved into an eerie grin.

"Eden?! You mean like Adam and Eve, Eden?" Willow asked in discomfort.

"Yes, yes, I remember those two.... such an unfortunate event." He slowly shook his head while straightening back up.

Willow was really confused now, and her heart sped up faster, afraid of the answer to her next question.

"So am I dead?"

"What do you think?"

"Well, I'm not quite sure."

"Well, yes and no. Come child, there is much before you, but first we must go back in order to go forward".

"WHAT?! That makes no sense and you really didn't answer my question!" Willow said, now very annoyed.

"Sometimes if you leave unfinished business in your past you will become stagnant, unable to fulfill your life's purpose." Dregus turned around and began to walk, waving his hand for her to follow. Dumbfounded, she quietly followed him down the riverbank. They came to a part of the river where there was a clearing in the land and a sturdy bridge reaching across to the other side. On the other side there was a path that went through a beautiful archway made up of vines and lilies.

Dregus whistled a dreamy tune that almost hypnotized Willow and immediately afterwards four horses stepped out of the bushes into the clearing. They proceeded in a line, one right after the other.

The first was pearly white and walked with an air, having its nose pointed up to the sky. He wore a crown made of pure gold on his head, playfully embedded with jewels. The second was of a fiery red, with striking flames glowing from its body. He had piercing beady eyes of rage and his nose was formed as a gun barrel ready to fire. The third was silky black, and his ears were fashioned like a weighing scale, reminding her of the judicial symbol for checks and balances. He looked horribly malnourished, with his ribs clearly visible. The last one had no true color at all, but he had pale muted skin that looked like ashes. He was slightly transparent, revealing all of his organs and the skeletal structure of his body. On one accord they all bowed down their heads and knelt on their front two legs before Dregus.

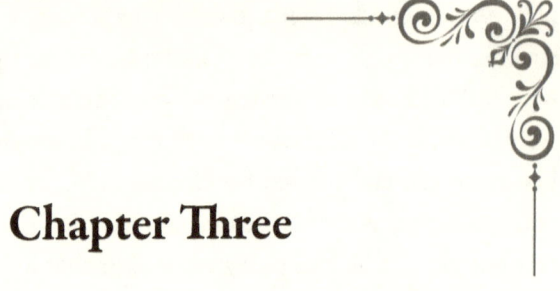

Chapter Three

Each horse carried a small satchel hanging from their saddle. One by one, Dregus went to each horse and grabbed something out of the bags, while whispering in their ears. Once he was done he snapped, waving the horses away, and they quickly obeyed. He walked up to Willow and said, "These are called accusers." He laid out his hand and Willow recognized them as the pebbles that she had seen on the floor of the river earlier. "They have much to tell," he said, as he took one pebble and swirled his hand around, while mumbling something in another language. She couldn't understand the words that were coming from his mouth, which made her very uncomfortable.

Then he tossed the pebble into the river, and when it hit the water, ripples started to form, growing bigger and bigger with each passing second. "Come child." He waved for her to stand next to him. Then, the water bubbled up as if it became boiling hot. Suddenly, the water settled, displaying a picture in the middle of the river. Shocked, Willow rubbed her eyes and then closed them for a second. When she opened them back up, she leaned forward to get a better view. She wasn't imaging things; the vision was still there in the water.

It was of her, back in her room, lying on the floor after she had taken the pills. "What is this? Is this some kind of game?" she shouted as she looked up at Dregus.

"I assure you this is no game. Is this not you? Did you not put *YOUR* fate into *YOUR* own hands? Is this not the last thing you remember before coming here?"

"No, not quite.... I don't remember them!" she cried, pointing back to the scene set in the river.

Around Willow's helpless body was a circle of dark, deformed creatures with muddy red, slimy bodies eagerly waiting for the command to attack. There was one out of the bunch that had ashy grey skin and was greater in size. The top of his head was shaped like a hook with a pointy sharp end and his shoulders matched his head, protruding up into razor sharp points. He was going berserk with rage because he couldn't get to her. There was no question in her mind that he was the leader of the pack and he wanted to tear her apart.

The only things protecting her were two yellow, pole-like creatures that appeared as glowing beams of light. They were positioned strategically in the center of the circle, facing their opponents. One stretched out it's gigantic wings around her, which were shields of mighty steel armor. They gave no leeway to the aggressors who were trying to penetrate the barrier. The other beam of light was much bigger, and had a muscular structure to its form. With the stance of a solider prepared for battle, his sword was drawn, sparkling in reflection of the being's own light. And, a thin red bubble that was almost invisible surrounded them as a reinforcement of their protection. Every time one of the evil creatures on the outside touched the bubble in an attempt to attack, they would scream out in pain and burn up in flames, leaving behind a puff of smoke.

SIMULTANEOUSLY TO WILLOW dosing off to her expected end, Petundan ran to her from his post, passing the snarling demons that surrounded her. Once he was right next to her, he spread out his wings, unleashing his armor to stretch the circumference of where Willow laid. The evil spirits swung and attacked him, biting him with their fangs and ferociously striking with long claws. The angel yelled out in pain from every blow and he began to question if he would be able to protect Willow on his own. Deep down he feared he would fail, for he was only a guardian. He wasn't trained for such a battle.

From behind the chaotic crowd, the large evil commander came forward, throwing all of the little ones out of his way left and right. He finally got close to the guardian angel and he glared in his face. Just then lightning struck in the room, knocking the demons down to the floor, and instantly another angel appeared. Petundan sighed in relief, because he was no longer alone in the fight. Michael appeared between Petundan and the infuriated commander and lifted one hand in front of his face saying, "Stop, Death you cannot come any further. I am sent with orders from the Head Chief Intercessor that sits at the right hand of the Father. You have no authority to take her."

"Yes, I do! She renounced her faith in Him and has taken her own life. She renounced her keys to His kingdom. According to the law, we have legal right to take this one. She belongs to the pit of eternal darkness." Death hissed as veins bulged from his neck and spit flung from his deformed mouth.

"The Lord of Hosts said no, and His word shall not return unto Him void. For now, the blood of the unblemished Lamb covers her and you have no power in this matter," Michael confidently retorted, with great authority.

Right after he released the word, a thin sheet of red blood formed a dome like force field separating Willow, Petundan, and Michael from the evil that controlled the rest of the room.

"Thank you for coming when you did, great warrior. I would not have been able to hold them off for long by myself," Petundan said with relief, now that the hedge of protection was in place. "Yes, friend, I came right when I was commanded. You have done well keeping her safe thus far. But it looks as though our work is far from over. It has just begun."

"AHHH, GET THEM AWAY from me!" Willow screamed. She turned to Dregus. "Do something!"

"There is nothing I can do. You have made your choice."

"What is that light that is protecting me?"

"Oh, that. Yes, that would be your angels, sent to rescue you," Dregus said in a low voice.

"Am I dead?"

"I do not understand.... why are you so distressed? Is that not what you desired?"

"No! I mean, yes... I mean.... I don't know what I wanted! I - I - I take it back. I take it all back. I don't want to die!"

"Yeah, I bet you don't. You never deserved life; none of you do. I don't know why He so freely gives it. None of you even appreciate it," Dregus mumbled while frowning up towards the sky. Willow bursted into tears, not knowing what else to do. He grabbed her arm. "Look at me," he shouted. She looked up with blood shot eyes and she trembled with fear. "Your life is hanging in the balance. You are in the shadow of death," he warned. "You must pay close attention, because what you do next determines your fate." Willow looked back at the image in the water, sending a wave of regret into her heart. *How could she have done such a horrible thing to herself? She was a fool.*

More dread came over her as she wondered where her eternal home would be. She knew that suicide was wrong, and that God had no tolerance for it. Why did she stop believing and trusting God? Now that her eyes were open to the truth of what was happening around her, she wished she had listened and taken heed to what her grandfather had been trying to tell her all along. Thinking back on the argument she had gotten into with him the day before, she was overwhelmed with shame.

———— ⟨♦⟩ ————

WILLOW LAID IN HER bed listening to music through her AirPods. Her door opened abruptly and she sat up, startled by the intrusion. Stephen, her grandfather, barged into her room, amped with a mission.

"Get up from there, young lady!" he said sternly. "Your mom called me over here because she says all you do is stay in bed day in and day out!"

"What is that woman complaining about now? I wish everyone would just leave me alone!" Willow pouted as she jumped off the bed onto her feet.

"Look, we are all worried about you. We've never seen you like this before. I know that you are upset about your friend, Louis being in the hospital. But we all are. Don't shut out the people who care about you the most. You need to change your attitude and trust in God. He's working it out."

"I am not bothering anyone, and when did my "mother" start caring about me anyway?! When I needed her the most she wasn't there and now that she got Jesus and all you would think she was Mother Teresa or something!" Willow yelled, stomping her foot down.

"I 'clare girl, ever since you went and dropped out of school, I don't know who you are anymore. You should be happy for your mother getting saved and changing her life around for you and your brother. I remember leading you in the sinner's prayer when you were ten years old; don't you still believe?"

"No, I don't! Your God took away my daddy, and my life has gone downhill since then. Your God allows bad things to take the lives of people He so-called loves every second of the day all around the world. What a phony! He sits back and watches us suffer and does nothing to protect us. So NO, I don't believe in your God! Don't you see how things keep getting worst for me? He's not workin' nothin' out!"

As she shouted those words, everything became very still and silent. She sat back down on the bed and turned her back to her grandfather.

Signaling that the argument was over, she put her AirPods back on. Stephen stumbled back in disbelief, shaking his head as he backed out of the room and closed the door.

PARANOIA ENTERED HER mind as she imagined the eternal damnation she would more than likely face. "There is more for you to see," Dregus said, interrupting her thoughts. He took another pebble and repeated the swirling of his hand, and then threw it into the water with greater force than before. This created a huge splash that extended high in the air. When the water settled, another image formed in the river. It was a man dressed in an army uniform, embellished with gold medals and a purple heart; he was standing at the end of a driveway holding a bag on his shoulder. He was looking straight ahead with a blank stare.

"Daddy!?" escaped Willow's mouth. She looked at Dregus and he said, "Pay close attention," nodding towards the water. Willow turned and watched one of the most painful parts of her life play before her eyes like a motion picture.

DAVID STOPPED AT THE driveway of his home, taking a deep breath before he walked up to the front door to face his family. He hesitantly rang the doorbell and cleared his throat. "Willow, come pick up your shoes that are......" Tammie's sentence dropped off as she opened the front door and saw her husband standing before her. Tammie screamed, "David, you're home!" Then she looked him up and down in horror at the sight of her frail husband. She was startled by the bandage wrapped around his head. "Hey, baby," David said with a broken smile. Dismissing her initial reaction, she jumped into his arms and began kissing him compulsively on his face.

Willow was picking up her shoes from the kitchen floor like her mom had begun to ask when she heard the commotion happening at the front door. She ran to see what all the fuss was about. Walking up, she saw the army green suit and instantaneously dropped her shoes and ran straight for who she knew was her dad. With tears in her eyes she clung tightly to his waist, making him stumble a bit. "Daddy!" she smiled.

"Not so hard, baby." He winced, letting Tammie go and grabbing his side. He extended a hand to his left leg as he almost lost balance. "Sorry, Daddy," Willow said as she stepped back. Now that she was close she had a chance to examine him, focusing in on the wounds on his face and head. "What's wrong with your side?" Tammie asked, reaching out with concern.

"I... I was shot there. The doctors say I'm healing up pretty good, but it's still pretty sore."

"Oh my goodness! Are you alright? And what about your leg?" Tammie asked in horror as she anxiously flooded him with questions.

"Calm down honey. I'm fine." David looked at Tammie with sorrow in his eyes, then looked down and pulled up his pants leg. She put a hand over her mouth and Willow grabbed her hand and began to cry. He had revealed the metal structure standing where his leg used to be. "It's ok, please don't cry, technology has come a long way and I have this cool prosthetic leg," he soothed, motioning for Willow to come closer. Willow slowly touched his fake leg and quickly pulled her hand back, afraid she might hurt him. David sighed and dropped his pants leg back down.

Tammie quickly changed the subject, "Well, we're so happy that you are home. Come inside, you must be exhausted from your long trip back. I will make you something to eat," she coaxed, holding back the tears. They all went inside, each processing conflicting feelings of sadness and joy.

Chapter Four

E ven though they were eating spaghetti for dinner, which was Willow's favorite, she was very quiet. She kept her head down and ate in silence. She just couldn't stand to see her father in his wounded state. Something wasn't right; she couldn't put her finger on it, but he was different. The change was beyond her father's fragmented body. She sensed that something had been altered within him.

"You've given us the greatest surprise, honey! We had no idea you were coming home. You didn't even mention it when we talked on the phone the other day. We have missed you so much, isn't that right Willow?" Her mother asked, making light of the heavy situation. Willow nodded her head up and down, making sure to keep her eyes on her plate. By now she was just playing with her food, poking it with her fork. "I am glad to be back, that's for sure. It is really bad over there in Iraq! All the years I have been in the service, I have never experienced anything like it," David said staring off into the distance, wandering away from them.

Tightly griping his fork, he rose up from his chair, "When we got ambushed shots were going everywhere, and my men were going down left and right. We were outnumbered, being that we underestimated their weapons and defense capabilities. Sargent Hancock went down right beside me; he basically died right in my arms! While I held him, I got shot in the head and side!" He picked up his fist with the fork and then slammed it on the table, making his glass of water fall over.

"Then the big explo..."

"David!" Tammie interrupted, and looked over at Willow, who was still looking down at her plate.

"May I be excused, mommy," Willow asked, startled. "

Yes baby, go ahead to your room and play," Tammie answered.

After Tammie was sure Willow had left and gone upstairs, she turned to David who was still raised up from his chair but was very distressed with confusion. He looked down and then burst out crying uncontrollably, realizing he had upset his family. "I'm so sorry! Look at me, I am such a mess," he continued hysterically. "I don't know what's wrong with me, I just..." He let out a loud wail of a cry. Tammie didn't know what to do; she had never seen her strong husband so broken.

"It's ok, honey; you have been through a lot. Just calm down please. You will frighten Willow." As a nervous reaction she went over to his side of the table and started to clean up the puddle of water on his side of the table. David stood all the way up and stepped away from the table. He was still wailing as he grabbed her roughly and screamed in her face, "You don't know the things that I've seen, innocent families separated, babies dead out in the street, little children forced to be killers, women mutilated in ways you don't even want to know!" He threw her with force and she fell back and landed on the floor. He lifted his hands and laid them on his head. "And the things that I had to do! You wouldn't believe. So don't you tell me to calm down," he yelled, shuffling anxiously around.

Then he started to mumble something she couldn't make out and hugged himself tightly. He dropped to the floor holding himself and rocked back and forth, continuing to mumble. Tammie watched the once courageous army hero being reduced down to a child in the fetal position on their kitchen floor. She did the only thing she knew, which was to call David's father, Stephen, and he prayed over them.

The next day Willow came home from school and found her grandfather sitting in the living room reading the paper. She dropped her book bag and ran to sit on his lap. "Hey, grandpa, I didn't know you were going to be here." She gave him a big hug. "Where are Momma and Daddy?"

"Your mom took your dad for a doctor's appointment...nothing major, just a checkup."

"Really, just a check up?" She gave him an 'I know I'm young but I ain't stupid look.'

"Look, baby girl, your dad has been through a lot. He is sick, and his sickness goes way beyond his physical wounds. It's up in here," Stephen pointed to his head.

"I knew it! When I saw him I knew that he wasn't the same and the way he was talking to Momma last night was really scary," she exclaimed.

"Well, he can and will be healed in Jesus name. We just have to pray and believe in the healing hand of Jehovah Rophi. Amen?"

"Amen!"

Just then Tammie and David walked in through the front door. "Hey Mommy, hey Daddy," Willow said while running to hug them both.

"Hey, sweetie," Tammie said.

"Hey," David said, and he nonchalantly hugged Willow when she came up to him. Then he walked like a zombie to the couch and plopped down, withdrawn from the world around him. Everyone stared at him for a minute and then Tammie turned to Willow. "Honey, run to your room and let me and your grandpa talk for a minute, ok?" Willow ran out the room, but stayed in the hallway, pushing herself up against the wall so she could eavesdrop on their conversation.

Tammie walked into the kitchen and motioned for Stephen to follow her.

"Dr. Graham said that he has a classic case of PTSD, Post-Traumatic Stress Disorder."

"I figured that when you told me what happened yesterday. Now, you telling me the service didn't know something was mentally wrong with him when they let him go?"

"At the VA clinic they say that a lot of times veterans fall through the cracks without the proper evaluation."

Shaking his head, he said, "So what are the treatment options?"

"Well, he is set with a physiatrist that he has to see twice a week and he is on antidepressants. They also gave him Valium for anxiety. He just took his medication before we came in, that is why he is so out of it." She began to sob.

"Are you ok?" Stephen asked.

"You know, I really don't know. It's like he is a complete stranger in his own home. Last night he was tossing and turning the whole night. Twice he woke up screaming, "No, not again," over and over while drenched in sweat."

"I'm gonna move in."

"No dad, you don't have to do that."

"I just don't feel that it is safe with you and Willow being here alone with him right now."

"We will be ok, trust me. If at any point I feel any different I will let you know." She grabbed his hand and squeezed it. "Thank you, Dad."

Willow had heard about as much of the conversation as she could take. She quickly stumbled upstairs to her room and tightly closed the door. She jumped in the bed and stuffed her face in her pillow, crying as hard as she could. She remembered the morning when her dad left. She strongly felt that he was not going to come back, that this time was going to be terribly different. Now she knew that she was right. Her father did not come back, and whoever this person was that walked through the door claiming to be him was an imposter. After she had no more tears to cry she prayed to the Lord like her grandpa had taught her;

"Heavenly Father, which art in heaven,

I come to you in the name of my Lord
and Savior Jesus Christ.
I thank you that you have blessed me by
bringing my Daddy back home, but Father God, he is sick.
I just pray that he will be touched by
your healing power.
Cover him and release him from his pain.
I believe that you are more than able.
For by the Stripes of Jesus he is healed,
In Jesus name Amen."

"WHY DIDN'T GOD HEAR my prayers? What did I do wrong? Why didn't God heal him?" Willow demanded, turning away from the river to Dregus.

"Is it not written to not set foot on the path of the wicked or walk in the way of evildoers, avoid it, do not travel on it; turn from it and go on your way," Dregus said throwing his hand in the air. "Seems to me he chose the wrong path."

"No, he was a solider of honor! He protected his country with selflessness and with the best intent," she shouted. Pacing the ground, Dregus held his hands behind his back, "Hmmm, maybe the dark hold on him from all that killing was too much." Then he nodded towards the river.

She turned to see the shell of a man assumed to be her father sitting slumped down on a recliner with the TV on, but not paying attention to anything on the screen. Standing directly behind him was a ghostly figure that wore a black hooded cape, concealing its face. From underneath the cape there were long green tentacles spreading out along the floor. They reminded her of the legs of an octopus rooted in the ground. One of the tentacles was wrapped around David's head and another was around his neck.

"What...what is that?" Willow stuttered.

"That, dear child, is a ruler of darkness. A malicious stronghold. His name is Despair and through his tentacles he gave your poor daddy a dose of hopelessness to the head, with a shot of depression in the neck, oh pity," he mocked in a childlike fashion.

"*WHAT*?! How could that be, we never saw that...that thing. I never saw any of this at the time!"

"Pity, pity," Dregus taunted while shaking a finger in her face. "Were you ever really His child? You do know that in the realm of time, which you came from, there is way more than what meets the eye. There were consistent wars between good and evil going on all around you the whole time. The things that your eyes were able to see took no precedence over what was really happening in the invisible."

"My grandpa would always quote that "the effectual and fervent prayers of a righteous man avails much." Why didn't our prayers help him? At least my grandpa's and mom's prayers should have caused some type of turnaround," she asked angrily.

"And who are you to say what should and should not be? Are you God? Anyway, trust me, what Satan had planned for your dad would have been a lot worse if not for your prayers," Dregus said with grimace on his face.

She turned to the image in the river and saw her ten-year-old self walking down the hallway toward the living room. She braced herself for what she knew was coming next.

AS WILLOW WALKED DOWN the hallway to talk with her father, she thought about how much of a rollercoaster everything had been ever since he came home at the beginning of the year. Six months had gone by and he was still so unstable. He was actually worse than he was when he first came home. Sometimes he would laugh and joke and he'd seem like his old self again. Other times the house was filled with shouting and frantic arguments he would instigate with her mom over the smallest thing. The nightmares had gotten worse, waking him two to three times a night. He would wake screaming so loudly that she just knew the whole neighborhood heard him.

Then he would go into peculiar moods where he would be completely silent, staring out into space for hours at a time. It became harder to get him to go to his therapy sessions and her mom was constantly fighting with him to take his medication. Tammie, unfortunately lost that fight most of the time. But nothing was worse than the days he would drink. He had found a new friend in alcohol, which contributed to his deteriorating condition. He started having intense hallucinations where crazy accusations would come out of his mouth. As time went by and his drinking increased those days became more frequent.

Willow's mom asked her to give her dad some space so he could heal up, and for the most part she had done just that. But she was fed up and increasingly upset about everything because she wanted her dad back. She felt as if God didn't care about him or the family because he wasn't getting any better. What a cruel game to play having her dad come back but in such a wounded condition. She told herself today she was going to spend some time with her dad and she alone would make him well again.

Chapter Five

On Willow's way down the hall she passed by the guest room. She saw her mom in her peripheral view and stepped back so she could look inside. Tammie was sitting on the bed smoking a cigarette. Willow had never seen her mother smoke before and her hand was shaking so bad that the cigarette barely made it to her mouth when she went for a pull. Her shoulders were slumped down and her whole body was shaking uncontrollably. Willow was shocked at the condition of her mom.

Tammie grabbed a bottle of pills, it looked like her dad's prescription, and she poured out two into her hand. She popped the Zoloft into her mouth and proceeded to wash them down with a glass of water.

"What's that, Momma," Willow pried. Tammie jumped, splashing the remainder of the water in her glass on herself and the bed.

"Oh honey, you scared me," she said grabbing her chest. "Mommy's just not feeling too well today, sweetie." she said apologetically.

"But Momma, you said smoking was bad for you," Willow pleaded.

Now aggravated Tammie yelled, "Willow, not now, go somewhere and play." She got up and slammed the door in her daughter's face.

Willow stepped back with hurt and confusion. Then she thought about it and realized that her mom had become secluded and she, also wasn't the same. She barely spent anytime with her anymore because all of her focus was on her dad. Her mother's rude response was far out of her character, even so, but Willow shook it off and continued on her mission. She knew that if her dad was well again everything else would go back to normal, so nothing was going to block her plan.

"Hey, Daddy," she said with cheer as she walked into the living room. David continued to stare in the direction of the TV, ignoring what Willow had said. She sat down on the chair beside him. "Look, Daddy, I still have my necklace! I took real good care of it and I even memorized the bible verse that's on it. You want to hear me say it?"

He sat still, unmoved by her words. Looking him up and down, she saw that he hadn't showered in sometime; he had been wearing the same clothes for the past three days. He hadn't shaved either; there was thick stubble growing around his jaw creating a five o'clock shadow on his face. She examined the table beside him and saw a bottle of alcohol, which was almost empty. Ignoring her observations, she continued, "Daddy what I really wanted to tell you is that on my birthday that just passed I accepted Jesus into my heart. Grandpa helped me in prayer; I'm saved, Daddy," she said with excitement. David looked at her blankly. "That's good baby," David said with no expression.

Then she saw it - his eyes. Before she didn't know what it was exactly that made her so uncomfortable to look at him, but at that moment the truth had been exposed. His eyes were different; they were empty without the glow she had always known, without life. Just then a loud sound came from outside that sounded like a gun shot. They both jumped in sync and David's face flinched. With a new wave of energy, he started to squat down to the floor. He crawled over to the window and peered out. "We are being ambushed, Hancock, come on we gotta tell the men to pull back!" he shouted franticly. He crawled on the floor from one window to the next. Looking at Willow, "Get down, Hancock, before you get shot." Willow, a little confused slowly peered out the window and saw a group of boys outside playing with fireworks in the street near their house. "Oh daddy, it was only some silly bo...

"Get down! NOW!" David screamed before Willow could finish her statement. Then a round of fireworks popped from outside one after another. She was shaking at this point, because David had pulled out a hand gun from his pants and slid against the wall aiming the gun towards the window. She couldn't believe her eyes, because she had overheard her grandpa telling her mother that he was going to get rid of all her dad's guns from out of the house. How he had managed to hang on to that one was beyond her.

"Daddy, it's me Willow. There's no one out there trying to get us. It was just fireworks going off!" By this time, he had big beads of sweat pouring down his face and was very jittery. He looked over at Willow as he squinted and yelled, "Hancock get down; we have to hide. You're gonna give away our location!" He did a 007 roll on the floor with no problems from his prosthetic leg, and grabbed the remote controller, talking in code.

"The egg has left the nest. I repeat, the egg has left the nest, over!" He put the controller up to his ear and waited a minute then proceeded to bang on it as if it didn't work. "Daddy!" Willow cried. He looked over at her and became very paranoid. "Who are you? Are you one of those child soldiers sent to kill me? Oh no you don't!" He pointed the gun up at her and Willow let out a low squeal. She was frozen in shock and terrified for her life. She couldn't believe that her own father had a gun pointed at her.

Tammie came running down stairs after hearing all of the commotion. She stopped and let out a scream, "David what are you doing? Drop the gun!" He stumbled getting up from the floor never taking the gun off of Willow. "No, those suckers are out there and they're using everything they got to get us. I'll be damned if I let 'em," he screamed.

"You have gone insane, you're not in the war anymore! You're at home with you family that loves you and right now you have a gun pointed at your own daughter! Put the gun down now," she ordered. He began to look all around the room shouting "Hancock, Hancock where are you?! Oh no, they've got him!" He was crying at this point, hitting himself in the head with the gun, "No, No, No!"

As he was distracted by his own delusions, Tammie lunged out towards him and went for the gun. They tussled for what seemed like ages, and then the gun accidentally went off twice. One bullet went through a window, shattering it into pieces and the other hit a lamp that was sitting on the side table, putting them in complete darkness. Tammie let out a grunt as he punched her in the stomach three times, with another punch in the face to follow. He hit her so hard that she flung across the room and hit the wall, knocking her out cold.

Willow remained frozen in the same spot with her heart on overdrive in her chest. She wanted to run to her mother to see if she was ok, but she couldn't move. By that time, the dominance of red and blue flashing lights of police cars flooded the room through the windows. Their neighbors must have called the police, hearing the gun shots that were fired. David hurried across the room, knocking Willow over and tripping over furniture that had fallen during the tussle. He finally made it to the front door and opened it, running outside, leaving it wide open.

"Drop the gun and put your hands up," one of the cops shouted at David. Willow ran to the door and peeped slightly out of the threshold to see what was going on outside. There were two cop cars parked haphazardly in their yard and four police officers were shielding themselves behind the cars with their guns aimed and ready to fire. Her dad was standing in front of the porch in the grass, pointing the gun carelessly, moving from one officer to the next. Tammie finally woke from the attack and limped out the door onto the porch. "David, drop the gun, please! It is ok. Everything is going to be ok! Just do what they say," she blurted. "Put down your gun, NOW!" Another officer shouted stepping out towards him. "Oh no, you don't. You stay away from me," David demanded as he took a shot at the officer but missed. Right after he pulled the trigger a bullet hit him right in the chest. The exchange happened so quickly that it put him in shock as he grabbed his wounded chest and dropped to his knees. Tammie ran up to him, screaming and crying like a mad woman. She grabbed him just as he was falling to the ground and cradled his head in her arms. "Oh baby, NO, NO, NO!" Tammie yelled over him while stroking his face. "Call an ambulance. Where is the ambulance!" she hysterically screamed back at the police.

Willow walked outside and got close enough to her parents on the ground to see that her father was still conscious, fighting for each breath he took. David looked at her and she saw his eyes. Yes, *his* eyes - those were the eyes she remembered. He had come back to himself; the glow of life was shining through.

Willow came a little closer to where they were on the ground. There was so much blood, it was everywhere. There was no way in Willow's mind that her father would make it through this. David looked at them both and tried to speak. "Shhh, baby save your strength," Tammie whispered as she put a finger over his mouth.

"I.... a...am...so.... s...sorry." He struggled for every syllable. Tammie cried uncontrollably as the ambulance pulled up to the street. David looked towards the sky and said, "Ppplease for...give mmm....me Lord!" Suddenly blood gushed out of his mouth and he choked, struggling for air. Just like that he was gone. That was the moment Willow was introduced to numbness.

WILLOW CRIED AS SHE watched her father take his last breath for the second time. Dregus moved closer to her. "There, there, child; he sowed and so he reaped." Willow ignored his comment and kept looking at the scene in the river and saw something she hadn't seen back then. A few moments after he took his last breath, a blinding ray of light shot up from her father's chest and Despair and all its tentacles disintegrated away. "Oh! That's enough of this part, let's move on," Dregus said quickly, and clapped once, making the vision cut to another scene.

"Wait, I wanted to see that. I need to see that! Where did he go? Where is he now? Can I see him?" she asked anxiously.

"What do I know, child? I am just a mere keeper of the garden. Besides, this is your story, not his."

Dregus pointed to a new picture that developed in the water. It was of her walking through the front door coming home from school. There was junk scattered all around the house. Piles of dirty clothes were in the middle of the living room floor and there were mountains of dirty dishes in the sink. Stains were engrained throughout the carpet; food crumbs were sporadically embedded its fibers. Willow remembered all too well those days in that nasty apartment. She fought the urge to fight with Dregus about her father's whereabouts and gave her attention over to the gloomy vision.

Chapter Six

A couple of years following David's death, Tammie had gradually become withdrawn and was careless about life as a whole. She had developed a very strong drug addiction that consumed every facet of her world. As her need for an escape grew, she turned from Valium and Zoloft to harder drugs such as heroine. And as heroine took her deeper into the rabbit hole, roots of resentment for her own daughter Willow dug deep in the depths of her altered perception. She blamed her daughter for what had happened to David, because she had told Willow to leave him alone. She believed that if Willow had just listened to her, her husband would still be alive. Tammie didn't want to feel that way, but she did, which struck her with depression and anger, feeding her addiction. She opened herself up to the streets and gained new friends who meant her no good. But she didn't care, just as long as she could get high everything was daisies. Her needs got so bad that every cent that she earned or received went to any drug she could get her hands on. She had already blown through most of the insurance money from her husband's death, which caused them to downsize and move into a two-bedroom apartment on the rough side of town.

Willow hated coming home every day after school. The worst part of it all was walking through the front door and being greeted with the mess that was always waiting for her. Willow tried to clean the place up, but no matter how much she did, it never lasted. She took long strides over all of the obstacles that blocked the entryway of the apartment.

Then she entered the living room to find her mother laying on the couch passed out.

An empty bottle of Whiskey was tipped over beside her. She had a cigarette lit in one hand and it was almost down to a nub. Willow hurried over, grabbed the cigarette out of her hand, and mashed it into the ash tray that was laying on the floor. Willow didn't even know why she bothered to use the ash tray. Her mother had conveniently made the carpet and couch into one with all of the ashes and burn holes all over the place.

Tammie was dressed in a short pink mini skirt and a white tank top that exposed her cleavage and navel. She had gone out partying the night before and hadn't bothered to change. It was the same thing day in and day out. All her mother cared about these days was partying and high. It was hard to believe how much of a complete 180 her mom had done now that her father was gone. It was like she was a completely different person. This scared Willow; she didn't understand how a person could change so much in just two years.

Tammie slept during the day, and at night she would come alive. Staying out past dawn became routine for her. So seeing her like this was the norm by the time Willow came home from school. Sometimes Willow would get up to get ready for school and her mother still wouldn't be home. Tammie had lost her job as head RN at the Memorial Hermann-Texas Medical Center because she was caught high while on the clock in the ER. She was stripped of her license and her whole career was shot down the drain for good. Nowadays food stamps and welfare were their main source of income.

Willow looked down at her mother with disgust and shame, she had lost both her dad and her mother all at the same time. As far as she could see, her mother had died too that day, and there she was abandoned all on her own. She shuffled through the maze of clutter and went to her room. When she entered her room, the necklace her father gave her, which was sitting on her dresser, caught her eye. She picked it up and read the first line.

"Blessed is the man that trusteth in the Lord."

"Ha, yeah right," she mumbled and flopped the necklace back on the dresser. She hardly ever wore the necklace these days, so most of the time it just laid on the dresser, rarely being noticed. Turning to face the elongated mirror that was hanging on the back of her closet door, she took a long look at herself with pity. Her appearance had gotten to an extreme low. She couldn't remember the last time she had really looked at herself. Her shirt and pants were dingy and old looking. They looked like hand me downs that barely fit her. Her mother almost never took her shopping for new clothes, or new anything for that matter. She was growing fast and there was just a small selection of clothes in her closet that she could still wear comfortably. She had cleverly put them in rotation day to day, but it wasn't long before many of the kids at school caught on. It became a common thing for her to get picked on in class. A group of boys in particular would call her a bum, pointing and picking at her beat up shoes, saying her feet were sanctified because they were "holy". As a daily ritual, she would run to the bathroom during lunch and cry the whole period right up until the bell rang.

Willow hated the way she looked, from her scrawny chicken legs to her thick curly hair that was always pulled back in a ponytail. She looked over at the model on the front of an Essence magazine on her dresser. *Why couldn't her skin be smooth and clear like hers,* she wondered as she played connect the dots with the pimples on her face. Though she was dissatisfied with much of her appearance, she did appreciate her bronze complexion, which was a gentle blend of her father's fair tan tone and her mother's deep mahogany brown skin.

Tired of looking at herself in the mirror, she went and sat on the bed with a sigh as she pulled off her sneakers. She reached down and rubbed her toes, which were sore to the touch. The pinky toes had corns on them because they were always compressed in shoes that were way too small. After massaging her feet and finding some relief, she slung her book bag around off of her back. Opening it up and turning it upside-down, she expelled all of the goodies that were hidden inside onto the bed. A new pair of jeans, a black and white polkadot dress, a pair of white sandals, a loaf of bread, and a big bag of potato chips all came tumbling out.

Since her mom couldn't care less about her needs being met and God had left her in this drought a long time ago, one day she decided to take matters into her own hands and she started to steal. It was her way out, the answer she had been looking for to escape the misery that followed her.

Willow shuffled through the bag, looking to find the item she needed most of all. With relief she pulled out a white bra and laid it with the rest of the clothes on the bed, unsure if it was her size because she had just grabbed what she thought was right in the store. She found out it was time for her to start wearing one because her guidance counselor at school had pulled her to the side and told her exactly that. She was full of embarrassment as her counselor told her things that her mother should have told her months ago.

Willow continued pulling items from her book bag. Left inside was a jar of peanut butter, a jar of jelly, and a candy bar. She had stopped by the grocery store to get some food on the way home, knowing that there would be no hot meal prepared for her. The only time her mom cooked anything and/or cleaned was when she knew the social worker was coming for a visit. Willow grabbed all of the food and went down stairs to the kitchen. Before walking into the kitchen she looked in the living room to see her mom still stretched out on the sofa. She laid everything on the kitchen table and went to the sink to clean the dishes. After she cleaned up the kitchen she looked in the refrigerator. It was completely empty inside except for half a gallon of milk and a carton of eggs. Willow wasn't surprised at all, as she reached in and grabbed the milk.

While she was making her a sandwich the phone began to ring. She quickly ran for it and picked it up. "Hello," she said almost out of breath.

"Hey, sweetie! You doing alright?" Stephen said on the other end.

"Grandpa!" she yelled with excitement.

"Who is that?" Tammie slurred as she sat up on the couch. Willow turned to look over at her mother and her heart began to quicken.

"That better not be your triflin' grandfather," Tammie snarled, stumbling up from the couch in Willow's direction.

"Willow, what's wrong? Is that your mother?" Stephen kept questioning on the other end. Willow remained quiet while staring at her mother; she didn't know whether to answer her grandpa or say something to her mom.

"I told you not to be talking to him, now didn't I?! Give me that phone right now," Tammie yelled as she snatched the phone from Willow's hand.

"Now you listen to me, you bastard! I told you to never call here ever again! You think you are just gonna up and take my child from me?! You think you can be a better momma than me, huh? Huh? Well, let me tell you one thing, dammit, you can't have her and you'll never see her or me again!"

"Tammie, honey, you're sick! You need help. Let me help you, please! At least let me pray with you," Stephen begged.

"You know what you can do? You can take all that sappy stuff and go feed it to the dogs 'cause I don't wanna hear it! You have the nerve to call CPS on me and tell authorities that I'm an unfit mother and you still tryna come around here like everything is alright! Oh hell no, buddy! And for the record I'm an excellent mother!" She moved the phone off of her ear and put it right in front of her mouth and screamed, "And you know what? You are dead to me, you hear that? Dead!" She slammed the phone on the receiver and turned to Willow.

"GIRL, you so hardheaded! I told you not to be talkin' to him. He's nothing but a two-faced backstabber! How he gonna call CPS on me? He's just trying to steal you from me. You want to leave me?" Tammie moved closer to Willow, squinting her eyes suspiciously.

"I wouldn't mind staying with him for a while, Momma. I miss him," Willow said softly.

"What? What did you say? I know you didn't say what I think you said. So you want to go and stay with someone who betrayed me and is trying to get me in trouble? I could've went to jail!"

"Well, Momma, you're hardly here, and look, there's never any food in the house. He's only trying to help us. All he wants is for you to get clean and then we can all be a family again," Willow said boldly.

"Get clean! I am clean. I don't have no problem!" Tammie looked Willow up and down.

"Momma, you're just not here anymore; ever since Daddy died you have forgotten all about me. This morning when I woke up there was blood all over my sheets and I was so scared but I quickly realized that I had started my period. I needed you but you were not here. I would have really like to have gone through that with you, by my side. Then when you are here, you're usually high and completely unaware of what's going on around you. You might as well not be here at all."

"What are you talking about, I'm here now ain't I?" Tammie said with blood shot eyes and scratching all over, ready for another hit. "I am a good momma dammit, you are just an ungrateful whore! You better be glad I want you to stay here with me, 'cause I could throw yo happy ass out! And what you doing getting your period now? You ain't even old enough for that!" Tammie said belligerently.

"Ma, I turned twelve on Monday; you forgot all about my birthday! Partying and drugs mean more to you than I do! No, the truth is, you're not a good mother! Not any...."

Tammie slapped Willow in the face before she could finish her sentence. Falling to the floor with a thud, Willow held her cheek where she had just been hit. She slowly started to get up off the floor, but a foot came and kicked her in the stomach, causing her to fall right back down.

THE TWO HEADED STRONGHOLD laughed with a hiss, watching in pleasure as its victim, Tammie, crumbled right in its hands. She was obeying all of its manipulative commands, which were venom, poisoning Tammie's character with mind control. The creature had two sides; one was pale chalky white and formed as a woman. She had long red hair that glowed with flames. The other side was in an image of a man. Its muscular frame was enormous compared to the other side. With a sledge hammer arm that popped with bulging veins. When the creature opened its mouth, sharp fangs appeared. Jezebel gave an elusive whisper in Tammie's ear compelling her to continue her erratic behavior.

Chapter Seven

"So you think you a grown woman now that you done got your period. Well, let me tell you somethin'; I am the head honcho in this house, and you ain't gonna talk to me like you ain't got no sense." Tammie kicked Willow again. This time when Tammie kicked her, it was like she put all of her anger she had for Willow that had been brewing inside, into the force of the impact. Willow yelled out and grabbed the side of her stomach and curled up on the floor crying.

"Now get up and go on to your room. I got some company comin' over tonight. I don't need you messing up my night," Tammie said as she stumbled away, mumbling under her breath, "She wants to leave, huh? I should just let her hardheaded ass go..." Tammie's voice faded as she left the room.

Willow couldn't believe what had just happened. She was used to her mother going off on her for no good reason, but she had never hit her like that before. Anger began to boil within her as she got up off of the floor. It seemed like her mother had kicked her with a supernatural strength that left her sore with pain. As she moved around, she grabbed her side, wincing in pain.

Willow hurried as much as she could to her room like Tammie had ordered. It was Friday and she hated Fridays. That was when her mother had her drug dealer boyfriend and junkie crackhead friends over so they could get high and drink all night long. Tammie had lost all self-respect; she would do any and everything Justin, her drug dealer, wanted in order to get a free hit. During those parties Willow would usually lock herself in her room and blast music loud enough to drown out the outrageous acts going on down the hall in the living room.

When she got to her room, she looked in the mirror and saw that there was a little blood on the side of her mouth from where her mom had slapped her. Then she lifted her shirt to see a slight bruise forming on her right side. She went to the bathroom and cleaned her mouth. The music and laughter were already starting to come from the living room. "Oh man, they're already here." She rolled her eyes and continued to clean herself up. Then she ran herself a bath in an attempt to ease some of the soreness in her side. If only she could soak away the bruises in her heart.

An hour later she got out of the tub and went to her room. She turned on the TV and cranked up the volume as loud as she could. As she was putting her clothes on, her bedroom door swung open and Justin stood before her.

ON EITHER SIDE OF JUSTIN stood an evil presence. One was ten feet tall, with the frame of a man. Its face was slim, with sunken in eyes and cheeks, like a skeleton. There were sharp black spikes all over his body and he wore a wide mischievous grin. The other was in the form of a black wolf, gnashing its teeth, with glowing red eyes. He had eight legs that stretched from him like a spider. It was Perversion and Rage, and they were on assignment.

"WHOA, WHAT DO WE HAVE here, pretty, pretty? I was looking for your mom's room to get some money she owes me, but I think I found something way better," Justin giggled deviously, looking her up and down and rubbing his hands together. Willow tried to cover up, placing her pants in front of her, because when he barged in all she had on was a T-shirt and underwear. He stepped in and closed the door behind him. "Come on sweetie, don't be shy. Momma owes a debt and it is time to pay up. I think you will do nicely." Willow was shaking her head and moving backward with every forward step he took.

"No, leave me alone!" she shouted, competing with the loud TV she had cranked up before she got in the tub. Then she screamed out again, but that was no good with both the TV and the music playing down the hall competing with one another.

Justin got angry, "Oh, I get it. You want to play hard to get. Ok, I like that." He lunged out toward her and she turned to run but tripped over her new sandals that were lying in the middle of the floor. He picked her up and threw her on the bed. Willow struggled to fight back, but with his strength and the pain she felt from the beating she got earlier, she was no match for him. He straddled on top of her, blocking every blow she gave. "No, no, please no," she shouted as she continued to fight to push him off of her.

"I got you now," he said, as he ripped her shirt off and pushed her hands down. Willow quickly looked around her to see if she could reach for anything that could be used as a weapon.

PETUNDAN WATCHED FROM his post in a bundle of nerves. He kept looking up and then looking back at the horrific scene taking place in Willow's room. It grew harder for him to watch as Perversion and Rage moved in to take advantage of Willow. He was anxious because he had to wait for the ok to intervene. "Please, where are the intercessors? Oh, please, Majestic Ruler, let me help!" As he pleaded a gush of wind came from the north carrying a whisper. "Don't worry Petundan, I will go and take care of this matter." Comfort immediately came over Petundan because Holy Spirit had arrived.

WILLOW SPOTTED THE necklace her dad had given her on the nightstand beside her bed, although she knew it had been sitting on the jewelry box on the dresser before. It looked a little far out of her reach and she opted not to even try. But she had to do something quickly while Justin was distracted, unbuckling his pants. A sudden wave of calming strength come over her and fear vanished; bravery took over. She took a deep breath, gave it all she had, and reached for the necklace, which was somehow much easier to reach that it had appeared.

HOLY SPIRIT SWOOSHED down into the room and instantly took control of the atmosphere. As Willow, reached for the necklace, He blew it right into her hand. Perversion and Rage trembled and yelled when they saw Him coming. With a blast of force, He drove them out of His presence.

WITH ONE SMOOTH STRIKE, Willow slammed the medallion into Justin's face, yanking it down the length of his cheek. This created a deep cut from his eye all the way down to his mouth. Justin screamed so loudly she was sure everyone heard him over the loud TV. Raising up from Willow on his knees, he held his face, with blood oozing through the cracks of his fingers. She quickly rolled off the bed and grabbed some clothes that were laying in her chair at her computer desk.

"I am going to kill you, bitch!" he screamed over and over again now rolling off the bed to the floor. She put the clothes on in a matter of seconds, ignoring the screeching pain in her side. Looking down at the medallion dripping with blood in her hand, she felt a new appreciation for the gift her father had given her. Shoving the necklace in her pocket, she grabbed some Nikes that were on the floor. While a multitude of thunderous footsteps were coming down the hallway

Willow opened her bedroom window and jumped out onto a nearby tree like she had done before on many occasions.

She climbed down the tree, and once her feet hit the ground she took off like a track star. She didn't look back, not even once. Where she was going was unknown to her. All she knew was she had to keep running. The harder she ran the more she realized she wasn't just running from Justin but she was running from her mother, and all the chaos that had happened in her life. Most of all she was running from herself, because she no longer wanted her life. She desperately wished she were someone else. After wandering around for about an hour, she headed for the safest place she knew, no matter how long it would take for her to walk there.

Stephen was praying deeply in intercession for Tammie and Willow when the doorbell rang. He looked over at the clock hanging on the wall. It was 12:00 AM and he wondered who could be at his door at that time of night. He walked to the front door and glared through the window. Once he saw the girl trembling on the other side, he rushed to open the door. "Grandpa," Willow sighed with relief and ran into his arms. Once she was cuddled in the safety of his embrace she let go, allowing the tears that were built up within her to released. Unable to stop her body from shaking, Stephen pulled her inside and closed the door.

He held her tightly, consoling her. "Willow, you came all the way over here by yourself? How did you get here? What happened, sweetheart?" Stephen tried to pull her away to look at her face but she tightened her grip and buried her face into his shirt. Willow didn't answer, she just cried louder. He pulled away from her again, this time with success and led her into the den. On the inside Stephen was going crazy with worry while horrible thoughts formed in his head. No matter how frustrated he was inside, he remained patient with Willow. He made sure to speak in a low, clam tone. Sitting her down on the couch, he asked, "Do you want some hot tea?" while stroking her hair. She looked up at him and shook her head yes.

Most of the night Willow poured her heart out to him. She told him everything that had happened, starting from when her mom had hung the phone up on him earlier that day. He vowed that he would take care of her and that she wouldn't have to go back there anymore. He was upset with himself for letting her stay there for so long in such ill conditions, but he had been hoping Tammie would come to her senses and go to rehab and take back control over her life. This time he wasn't backing down, because he had more than enough proof from the bruises decorating Willow's side.

After that night Willow moved in with her grandfather. He had a talk with Tammie and by the end of the conversation she agreed to let him take her in because she was angry at Willow for messing up Justin's face. She didn't believe that he had tried to rape her. Instead, she believed Justin, who told her Willow had tried to force herself on him. She would believe anything he said just to keep her reliable source for her filthy addiction.

Chapter Eight

Right when the scene in the river vanished, Willow franticly demanded, "Why?! Why were those evil things around my mother and Justin? What does all of this mean?!" She wiped the tears from her eyes. Without a word Dregus pulled out the third accuser and slung it into the water, which created a whirlpool in the river. "I don't want to see anymore. I can't take it! I already had to live it once. Why do you want me to relive it again?!" Willow cried with anger.

"Oh, but you must child. You see, you expect me to just tell you what's going on and to give you all the answers. But it doesn't work that way. You have to see these things from a different perspective, the truth. You must see the full picture, and this requires you to see all the hurt, all the pain, and all of your ugliness. This is the only way you will get the answers that you desire. You are almost to the end. Wouldn't you like to see what it shall be?" he said with an intrusive stare and a smile on his face, "I know I can't wait!" His eyes widened. The whirlpool settled and another picture popped up, of her and her friend Nicole eating lunch in the food court of The Galleria Mall.

Now fed up, Willow shouted, "NO! I am not watching this any longer. This stuff actually happened to me! It's not a movie for you to play whenever you like for your own entertainment! You're not even helping me. I refuse to carry on with this silly game. I AM DONE!" Willow turned and proceed to walk away in the other direction, back into the enchanted forest. She picked her pace up to a run, but didn't get very far because she slammed into an invisible wall that blocked her way. The strength of the impact sent her sailing through the air and she hit the ground, sliding from its force.

It took her a minute to recover and get her head around what had just happened. She laid there in confusion because she couldn't see what she had come into contact with. There was nothing there. Looking back at Dregus, she saw his claw up in the air and his eyes rolled in the back of his head. He had created the invisible wall, blocking her from moving forward. He dropped his hand down and came back to himself. Walking over to where Willow grovelled on the ground, he spoke. "I assure you this is no game. Where do you think you're going? Look around, there's nowhere else for you to go! It would behoove you to stay and see what the stones have to show. I am telling you the truth when I say that your life depends upon it." He slowly leaned down over her and his voice became deeper. "You will get up now and face yourself! No more running, Willow! NOW GET UP!" he yelled. Willow jumped to her feet, now feeling threatened. She knew better than to get on Dregus' bad side, for she didn't want to see what this being was capable of. She walked back to the river and braced herself for what was next.

THINGS QUICKLY TURNED around for Willow when she began to live with her grandpa. Her life was almost normal. She was doing a lot better in school and now that she was in the eleventh grade it was very important, because the possibility of college was actually opening up to her. On the track she had been on before, no one expected college to be an option for her. Now, she was making a good impression in school and she was well liked, even a little popular with her peers. Long gone where the days when she got picked on about what she wore. She was blossoming, taking pride in her appearance. Even though she still struggled with her self-esteem, she hid it behind the fancy clothes and possessions she acquired through the habit she couldn't shake, stealing.

Before long, she began to think of stealing as an art form. There was a certain strategy to it that she had mastered that seemed to never fail her. Stealing had become so easy for her; it came second nature to her. This talent was all due to her best and only friend Nicole Burton.

Nicole was a self-proclaimed cold-hearted kleptomaniac. She taught Willow all she knew in the technique of getting whatever you want for free. After-school twice a week they would go to the mall and have a field day. Those were the few times that Willow was able to let loose and have a good time.

Her grandpa kept her on the straight and narrow, or at least he tried. He took her to church every Sunday, but she wasn't interested like she had been when she was a little girl. Willow didn't complain, because it made her grandpa happy, so she was happy too. But no matter how good things got for her, she couldn't shake the beast; she just could not stop stealing. She wanted to, but she loved the rush it gave her too much. She had become an addict just like her mother and stealing was her drug. It didn't help that her best friend Nicole encouraged her itch by being the queen of thieves.

"Hey, are you texting Louis again? Yuck! You guys make me sick," Nicole teased, sticking her finger in her mouth with her tongue out like she was about to throw up. Willow laughed and put her phone down. "No, I was letting my grandpa know that I would be home around nine."

"Oh.... anyway, I don't even know why you're dating Louis. Now, Brandon on the other hand, you know that's on the football team, looks way better and I heard he likes you. Besides, Louis is a goody two shoes, didn't you meet him in church or sumin'? Girl, I need a guy with some edge!" Nicole said flipping her long dark hair to the side.

"Well he is *my* boyfriend and I like him just the way he is. Anyway, if you like Brandon you date 'im." Willow proclaimed with a bright smile. Nicole lifted her hands in innocence. "Alright, alright just messin' wit ya. You have a boring relationship if you want to."

They continued to eat their lunch in the food court of the mall. "Anyway, what did you get out of Macy's?" Willow asked.

"Nothing, they didn't have anything I wanted."

"WHAT? Macy's has the cutest clothes! What do you mean there wasn't anything you wanted?"

"Nothing, I don't know. I'm just not in the mood."

"Wait what, am I dreaming right now? Did you just say you're not in the mood?!" Willow chuckled in surprise.

"Look, I'm just bored. We do this type of kiddy stuff all the time! We are grown now; I mean we're sixteen now, aren't you ready for something new?!"

"I don't really know what you mean Nicole. It sounds like you're losing it."

"Come on, girl, get with it. I am tired of stealing stuff that don't mean nothin'. It's time to get paid."

"What?" Willow was confused.

"You will see. I have been thinking about this for a while now and I have a plan to take us to another level."

Nicole smiled and got up from her chair. "Follow me," she giggled.

"I am not going anywhere with you until you tell me what we are doing." Willow didn't flinch from her spot.

"Ugh, come on Willow, stop being such a wimp. Man, you are being so lame right now!" Nicole slapped her hands on her hip, revealing her petite frame under her oversized shirt that draped over black leggings. "I promise you it will be the thrill of your life!" Nicole snapped around and started to walk away. Willow got up and reluctantly followed Nicole out of the mall to the parking lot. "I give, where are we going?" Willow asked as she stopped at the passenger side of Nicole's car and placed her hands on her hips. "It's a surprise," Nicole said sarcastically as she got into the driver's side.

About ten minutes later they pulled up to a deserted gas station that stood alone on a corner nestled in a group of trees. Nicole suspiciously looked around the whole area with sweat trickling down her face. Willow looked around too, not really knowing what she was looking for. But she wanted to see what the big fuss was about. Nicole remained extremely quiet and reached for her purse that was on the floor behind her chair.

"What are we doing here, Nicole?" Willow nervously questioned.

"Hold your horses; you will see in a minute." Nicole responded as she looked through the rearview mirror.

"Come on, I am ready to go. It is already past 8:30. I will need to be home soon! My grandpa will be ringing me nonstop!"

"Stop whining, ya big baby."

Nicole started to dig in her purse and pulled out a small pistol. Willow's eyes widened when she saw the gun. "What are you doing with that? You are seriously doing the most right now!"

Nicole held the gun tightly in her hand and kept looking around. "Alright, here's the deal, we go inside and I'll hold the cashier up with this while you go behind the counter and get all of the money out of the cash register." She threw a small cloth bag into Willow's lap "Put the money in this bag, and here, put this on," she said, throwing her a black mask. "Wait a minute! I am not going to hold this place up. This is too much, Nicole. What have you been smoking?" Willow said fearfully.

"Ugh!! Why do I put up with you? LOOK, we get in and get out quickly and no one gets hurt. Oh, and don't worry, I got one for you too," Nicole said with a smile as she pulled out another gun and held it out. Willow shook her head no. A phobia of guns had grown in her ever since the incident with her father. "I don't want that, get it away from me, NOW," she screamed.

"Shhh, keep your voice down. Look, you don't have to take the gun if you don't want to. I'm sorry if I seem a little pushy but I just wanted us to do this together, ya know? To have a little fun doing something more adventurous. I promise nothing is going to happen. Look, it's not even loaded." Nicole opened the chamber of the gun to show her that there were no bullets inside. "We will be on the phone tomorrow laughing and joking about how great it was. Plus, I didn't want to tell you this, but I really need the money. My mom lost her job about two months ago and things are getting tight. I need to get money for rent or we will be getting evicted."

"Why didn't you tell me? You do know that some people work to help their parents out, right?"

"It's too late for that. Our rent is due tomorrow and the landlord is not accepting any more excuses. Look, Willow I am tired of talkin', are you in or out?"

They stared at each other for a while and then Willow let out a sigh and snatched the gun out of Nicole's hand, putting it into the pocket of her jacket. Then she slid the black mask over her face. "Yes! See now that's why you my girl!" Nicole yelled. "We better not get caught," Willow said. She didn't want to admit it, but as they prepared to go in the store she felt a boost of adrenaline rushing through her veins. That high that she knew so well had intensified with the new level of danger awaiting ahead.

They sat and watched the attendant of the store through the windows. The little white guy behind the counter looked like he was in his early thirties. He sat clueless of the scheme being formed against him as he quietly watched the small TV on the shelf. Nicole thoroughly scanned the area one more time as a car slowly pulled out of the driveway of the lot. Once the parking lot was completely empty, she said, "Ok this is it. We got this, just remember the plan. I'll do all the talking, alright? Now, let's move out on three; One.... Two.... *THREE*!" They popped out of the car and ran across the empty parking lot into the store. Nicole led the way, busting through the double doors.

She had her gun pointed straight at the cashier. "Move from behind the counter and put your hands up!" He put his hands up and started to plead, "Please, please don't shoot! Whatever you want you can have. Please, please..." He didn't move. "Come on, we don't have all night.

Didn't I tell you to come out from behind there? What are you, stupid or something?" she shouted as she shot the wall beside him and then pointed the gun back on him. Willow jerked when the shot was fired and looked at Nicole in shock. Nicole had told her that the guns were empty. She wondered when she had found time to load her gun without her noticing. Willow's high came down and worry mixed with fear set in. *This girl is really crazy,* she thought.

The cashier jumped and bent his head down with his hands still up. "Oh no, please don't kill me," he cried.

"Open up the register and come from behind the counter! I am not going to say it again," Nicole shouted. He opened the register and moved from behind the counter while Willow watched. "Come over here and get down on the ground." Nicole ordered the cashier, and he obeyed. Willow couldn't believe what they were doing. It was like at that moment she came back to herself and regretted agreeing to do something so stupid. *How did she get sucked into this anyway?* she thought. "Hey, hey, hey," Nicole waved at her. "You forgot how to move? This is where you come in, remember? You better not screw this up!" Willow regained her will to move and walked behind the counter, shaking, and stared at the money in the register for a minute. As she put the money in the bag she saw a flashing red button going off under the counter top. "Oh no! He pushed an alarm to call the police! We've got to get out of here!" Willow ran from behind the counter with the bag of money in her hand.

Nicole began to walk slowly backwards towards the door and she tucked the gun into her pullover. At the same time Willow was moving from behind the counter, the cashier ran and dove behind the counter to grab his gun that was tucked on a bottom shelf. He stood up and start to shoot aimlessly. He hit Willow in the leg, causing her to fall screaming to the ground. "Shit," Nicole said, then in a panic she ran back to where Willow fell and yanked the bag out of her hand and ran out the door while he continued shooting. Willow laid still while the mad man fired his last bullet, each time missing Nicole as she ran across the parking lot. Willow found some strength, got on her feet, and quick shuffled out the door after Nicole. As she stepped outside, she saw Nicole get into the car and skid off without a second thought. "Wait for me," Willow yelled as she stumbled in the direction of the car.

The cashier ran out of the store chasing after Willow, "Where do you think you're going? Come back here!" Then she heard the police sirens that were getting closer with every second. She tried to hop away as she reached down towards the wound that was in her leg. She didn't get very far before the cashier caught her and held her hostage until the police came.

Chapter Nine

"So why did you feel the need to steal?" Dregus asked turning to Willow. Willow was ashamed "I don't know; it was all my mother's fault; she didn't care for me.... she left me alone! I needed things, I mean I was getting picked on at school. Then the robbery... I really didn't want to do it!"

"So why did you go along with something that you did not want to do?"

"I.... I don't know. I felt pressured to do it. I didn't want Nicole to feel like I wouldn't help her situation."

"But you knew it was wrong, right?"

"Well, it was all Nicole's fault!"

"Oh, how easy it is to point your naughty little finger at someone else, hmmm?! You made the choice, child," he roared. "That is the trickery of free will. No matter what you experience, you are always left with the power of choice, and what a deceitful power it is. Most of the time you humans are blinded by the troubles of life, giving evil access to manipulate you. Then you all forget about the fact that you can simply choose higher than what your present situation may look like. I've got a secret for you." He moved in closer to her and whispered, "There really aren't any limits in the realm of time. The limitations that you think constrain you are all illusions that are formulated by your own low level of thinking. And so, unfortunately, here is another bad choice which you made that you must face." He waved his hand and the picture in the river skipped forward to an image of her siting at the kitchen table eating a bowl of cereal.

WILLOW ATE HER CEREAL in silence as her grandpa came into the kitchen. A month had passed since the robbery and her grandpa had become stricter on her ever since. He hardly let her out of his sight and there was a silent tension between them. He walked over to the kitchen table and pulled out a chair to sit down across from her. He looked at her for a moment with disappointment. She kept eating, ignoring his stare. He rubbed his hand over his salt and pepper hair and let out a loud exhale. "I still can't believe you robbed that store. Why, Willow? Why did you do it?" he asked with sadness in his eyes. She continued to eat in silence. "I have tried so hard to give you a good peaceful home. Why are you stuck on throwing it all away? Don't you know you could have been killed out there? You should be thankful that the bullet only grazed your leg."

"I don't know, Grandpa, I'm sorry. Like I told you before, I just got caught up in it all."

"You don't just get caught up in nothing, girl! You chose to do it! I don't know what to do anymore," he said with his head down in defeat.

"Grandpa I'm sorry, I have stopped stealing and I have paid my debt. What else do you want?! I messed up, okay? And I have learned my lesson!" She didn't understand why they had to keep going over the same thing. It seemed like he would bring it up each and every day.

"You know you got off lucky with a year probation with community service. You are really supposed to be in a detention facility or even prison! You committed a felony. Armed robbery, and you had a stolen concealed weapon on you when the cops caught you, at that! You better thank the Lord for my District Attorney friend that owed me a favor. You got off really easy. But that friend of yours wasn't so lucky."

"She's no friend of mine. She deserves to be locked up somewhere," Willow said with a disgusted look on her face.

"If she tries to look for you when she gets out, I want you to stay away from her, ok?"

"You don't have to worry about that! She is nothing to me. I still can't believe she left me there all alone, to take the fall for something that she pressured me to do. How could she do that, especially after I got shot? She was never really my friend."

"Alright good, I'm glad you realize that. Now, I have someone coming over to see you, so straighten up." he snapped.

A few minutes after he said that the doorbell rang. "They're here," he said in a chipper voice. He rushed off down the hallway to answer the door. Willow listened intensely to hear the conversation taking place at the front door. "Hey! I'm glad you were able to make it. Look at you! You look so good," he said. A woman's voice came next.

"Hey! I have missed you so much. You look good too," she said as they hugged.

"Well don't just stand there, come on in. Make yourself at home!" Stephen exclaimed. Willow noticed how they talked as if they were old friends, separated and now being reunited. She tried to listen closely to see if she recognized the voice, but it was raspy and frail sounding. It was not familiar to her.

"Ok!" the woman responded.

"Here, let me take your coat." Stephen reached for her coat as the woman stepped into the foyer of the house.

"Ok.... where is she?"

"She's right down the hall in the kitchen."

Willow heard the clacking of heels hitting the hard wood floor with every step the woman took. As the visitor got closer Willow wondered who was so interested in seeing her. Coming through the doorway of the kitchen stood a woman with her hair neatly pin up in a classic bun, her face painted with makeup that was flawless. She wore a simple but elegant navy-blue dress that loosely fell right below her knees and was beautifully embroidered at the hem. She had on black high heel sandals with a fresh pedicure. This woman was put together from head to toe. "Mom, is that you?" Willow gasped with surprise. She got up from the table and got closer to get a better look. "Yep, it's me baby." Her mother now holding her arms out for a hug. Willow looked examined her mom closely. "I can't believe it, you look...." Then she turned her back to Tammie and said, "...different." Her mother was no longer the skeleton body with sunken eyes and unruly hair like she remembered. Tammie dropped her arms and cleared her throat. "Yes baby, I have changed a lot. I've changed for the better."

Willow really didn't know how to react to seeing her mom again. This was the first time she had seen her mother in five years. She really had no idea how she felt seeing her again. She was numb, and it consumed her in the moment, making her responses cold.

"Well look at you! My goodness how you've grown into a beautiful young lady. Where has all the time gone?"

"Probably down your crack pipe," Willow snapped.

"Willow, don't you dare be rude to your mother! She has turned her whole life around. I don't care what you think of her; she is still your mom. Besides, everyone deserves a second chance!" Stephen said from the doorway where he had been watching their whole encounter. Willow crossed her arms over her chest and rolled her eyes. Tammie turned to him and said, "It is ok, Dad. Let me talk to her alone for a minute." He backed away and left the room, respecting the fragile moment. Tammie walked up to her daughter and laid a hand on her shoulder, but Willow flinched away.

"Please don't touch me right now."

"Ok fine, we can go slowly. I completely understand." Tammie walked over to the kitchen table and sat down in a chair. "Come sit down with me for a minute."

Willow remained standing with her arms crossed tightly, ignoring her mother's request. Even though the woman before her looked and acted differently, she didn't trust her. She couldn't let her guard down; not even for a minute.

"So I heard you got into a little trouble."

"OMG! I know that is not why you are here! Oh, okay Tammie, so what you gonna try and be a momma now, huh? Please, if you have come to lecture me just save it, 'cause your words have no validation with me, okay?!" Willow challenged, looking straight into Tammie's eyes.

"Ok Willow, I deserve that. I don't expect you to run into my arms and tell me how much you miss me. I really did make a mess of things and I am so sorry. I just didn't know how to go on without your father. He was the love of my life. The rock that kept me grounded."

"Right, you have all of these excuses! But what about me, Momma? Didn't you feel a need to continue living for me? I needed you most of all then. After all, I lost Daddy too! Why did I have to lose you, too?"

"I know baby, and I am truly sorry. To be honest, I know this isn't gonna make sense and it may upset you, but I was so illogical that I needed someone to blame. And unfortunately, I blamed you for what happened." A multitude of tears cascaded down her mother's face.

"What? You blamed me? I was just a child who wanted her father to be well again," Willow said in a low tone as she began to cry.

"I know baby, and I am sorry. I wasn't thinking right." Tammie dropped her head. "But thank God for your grandfather, though. He would not stop bothering me and praying for me. Even after he took you in. He still would not leave me alone. I know that's why I am still alive to this day."

"Is that why you didn't believe me, Momma?! When grandpa told you what Justin tried to do to me? Why didn't you believe me and come to my rescue?!" Willow pleaded angrily, searching for an answer.

"Oh baby! I was all messed up. That woman before wasn't really me. It was the drugs and the depression that ruled my life. I didn't care about anything anymore. Honestly, I needed deliverance by the Lord's mighty power because I just wanted to escape the pain I felt and the drugs helped me do that! Half of the things I did or said I only faintly remember honey. I do believe you, because if he actually did it to me, why wouldn't he try to take advantage of you. You know what? After that happened Justin beat me so bad, I had to go to the hospital. When you started living with your grandfather my life went from bad to straight hell. Justin made me do horrible things that I can't even talk about right now. He said that I had to pay up for what you had done to him. It was like I was his slave. I don't know why I didn't go to the police. The drugs just had me bound. I spiraled out of control with no direction and no reason left to live. About a six months ago he got locked up for life on a first-degree murder charge. That is when I was able to get clean, or at least try. So my new life journey began. I struggled along the way, but your grandfather helped me a lot. The woman you see before you didn't happen overnight and I am happy to say that I have been sober for the last four months. The longest I have been clean so far. And look, God has made sure I stay sober too!" Tammie said, standing up cuffing her belly with her hand to reveal a small baby bump. "You are going to have a little brother!"

Willow looked at her stomach, then back to her mom's big grin. She didn't know what to say. Her mom was going on with her life without her. It was like she was meeting this woman for the first time. "Well, good for you Momma." Willow was unenthused, but truthfully seeing her pregnant angered her. She felt that the real reason her mother was getting herself together was because of this new child. Like she had forgotten all about her. There was a long silence. "Look, your grandpa told me about the trouble you got in and I knew I just had to see you. Honey don't throw your life away just because of my failures.

You are young and still have so much to live for. You have time to turn things around. I want to be in your life. Let me make this right."

"It's too late. There is so much that has happened, Ma. I don't think I can move past it," Willow said, and then stormed out of the room.

Willow's year-long probation went by quickly due to her focus on school and her desire to make her grandfather proud. Her mother continued to call her trying to build a relationship with her, but to no avail. She still didn't want anything to do with Tammie. She pretended to try to tolerate her mom just to appease her grandpa. When her mother gave birth to her brother, she wanted Willow in the delivery room right beside her, but she refused to go. Willow didn't like how she never mentioned anything about the father. When she would try and ask, Tammie would always weasel out by changing the subject. Willow hoped it wasn't Justin, but knowing how twisted her mother's mind was she wouldn't put it past her. Just thinking about everything that happened made it impossible for her to forgive her.

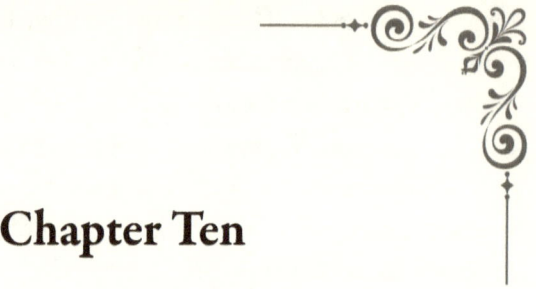

Chapter Ten

Willow graduated from high school with honors, among the top of her class. She had taken an interest in becoming a lawyer and was accepted to study political science at the University of North Carolina - Chapel Hill on a full scholarship, thanks to her exceptional SAT scores.

It was orientation day at Chapel Hill and Willow was filled with excitement siting in the crowded student union auditorium. Nothing could top the smile on her grandpa's face who sat beside her. He was overjoyed, because he had never thought that day would come. In his eyes it was truly a miracle, a great demonstration of how the Lord can turn your life around for the better.

There was a feeling of pure electric energy weighing thick in the room and playful banter going on amongst the bright shining faces awaiting the beginning of the introductory session. "You know, your dad would be so proud of you," Stephen whispered to Willow, squeezing her arm.

"Yeah, I wish he could've been here," she said with a little disappointment.

"I know, sweetheart, but he is here - in there," he said, pointing to her heart. "And hey, I see that you are wearing the necklace he gave you!" He grabbed the medallion.

"Yeah, it has helped me in more ways than one, and I thought I should wear it for today," she said, looking down at the necklace.

A woman finely dressed in a tan business suit with a black trim and black pumps walked on stage. Her hair was strawberry blond and wavy, coming down to her shoulders. She looked like she was in her mid-fifties, but time had been kind to her. With a distinguished air that told of her importance and sense of purpose, she walked up to the podium that was aligned front and center on the stage, causing the room to became quiet and still. She commanded the attention of the audience just by her mere presence. "Good afternoon, ladies and gentlemen, or should I say our great freshman class of 2009," she said with a gleam, and the crowd roared with applause. After a minute or two, "Alright, alright, settle down, settle down," she said with a pleasant smile, and the room was restored to its attentiveness.

"To properly introduce myself, I am Chancellor Judy Ferguson and I am proud to say that you all have made the right choice. The home of the Rams, the home of the Tar Heels, the home of the victorious! I am very proud to say that The University of North Carolina - Chapel Hill is my alma mater and I was groomed here and the will to succeed was embedded in me through this wonderful learning environment. I was once right where you are now. I remember the blood rushing through my veins, a cocktail of fear and excitement, not knowing what to expect. I also remember the satisfaction of independence being graciously given. You have so much to look forward to and so many people around you that are strictly here to help and guide you along the way. Please take advantage of this time of your life, because you'll never get it back. Now, time for a brutal truth that you will hear a lot your first few weeks. Look to your left; now look to your right." Everyone obeyed and started to look at the persons next to them. "Take a good look - one of you will not make it to graduation. Let this statistic be motivation for you to excel and use the many resources provided, so that you are more than guaranteed to make it to graduation in four years. With this great group being the School of Political Science, we expect a high level of excellence coming from you all. Our future judges, lawyers, and government officials will come from amongst you and we know that you are the best. The sky is no longer the limit. Now, I would like to take the pleasure of introducing you to your department chair, Dr. Daniel Morrison."

There was warm applause as a tall, slender man walked up to the podium. He was dressed in a tailored Armani black suit with a black tie. He had black hair and deep hazel eyes with a hint of green. A dimple appeared in his right cheek when he smiled revealing his strong muscular jaw line. He had a medium build and you could tell that working out was a part of his daily regimen. Willow and every other girl in the room took notice of how handsome he was, some gasping and whispering at the sight of him. His walk captivated her most of all. Every step was confident and smooth, as if he were gliding.

When he got to the podium, he shook Dr. Ferguson's hand and then took charge of the microphone. "Hello, freshman class of 2009! Like the esteemed Chancellor has stated, I am Dr. Morrison, and I am not going to sugar coat anything for you. That is one thing you will learn about me. This journey you are about to take will be tough along the way. You don't become a world changer just by slipping through the cracks. You have to work for it. You will have some wins and you will have some failures. Nothing is going to be handed to you. The ones who make it to the end are the ones who are able to learn from the failures and become better because of them. I am here along with your professors and counselors to give you guidance along the way, but you will be tested. How much do you want it? Are you willing to go the extra mile? Are you willing to say no to your friends that want to party so that you can spend more time studying for that exam? Again, I ask, how much do you want it? How far will you go to get it? This road is the one less traveled, and it's not for the weak of heart. Make up your mind today, no, make your mind up right now that you are going to stay the course! Welcome future world changers, welcome!"

As he finished his last sentence Willow started to fidget, because it looked like he was looking straight at her in the third row. She had to catch her breath as the crowd shifted into a rambunctious applause filled of shouts and whistles. It was just her imagination of course, but a girl can dream, can't she?

After all of the speakers were finished with their greetings to the freshman class, everyone was released to explore the campus and find their dormitories to unpack. It was a whole new world for Willow, a fresh start. For the first time since her father died, she was truly happy and expecting greater for her life. She stood outside with her grandpa by his car in front of her dorm after meeting her roommate Megan and unpacking a little.

Willow inhaled the cool, crisp, clean air. The sun was setting and the campus was scattered with people walking and mingling all around. "I can't believe I am here. It feels like a dream," Willow said, watching the people interact with each other. Stephen wrapped his arm around her shoulder. "You are in the big leagues now kiddo! Words can't express how proud I am of you. You're going to do great things! I just know it;" He took her hand in his, "believe it."

"Grandpa, do you think I can really be a good lawyer?"

"I know you will be great at anything you want to be. I never thought you would want to do something with law with your history and all, but you are full of surprises. This is your land of opportunity right here. All you have to do is stay focused and don't let anything or anyone distract you, especially Louis, you understand?" he asked, squeezing her in his arm with a big grin.

She and her boyfriend Louis had been together ever since the tenth grade and they were still going strong. Willow really cared for him and appreciated him for sticking with her during the whole ordeal she had gone through with Nicole, becoming a criminal and all. She was fortunate enough to have been able to go to the prom with Louis, and he took that time to profess his love for her. And even though they were going to different schools after graduation, they had decided they were going to try a long-distance relationship. She told herself if they could withstand the distance barrier and stay together through it all, then they were meant to be.

Willow giggled at her grandpa's remark. "Yes sir! I will do my best." She gave him a big bear hug.

"Now it is time for me to go, and let you soar like an eagle! I don't want to do it, but it must be done." He turned away to open the car door. "Oh wait, I almost forgot!" He dug into his pants pocket and pulled out a folded envelope. "Your mom wanted me to give you this. I don't know what it says, so don't ask," he said as he handed her the letter. Willow looked at it resting in her hand with a blank stare.

"Well, it ain't gonna bite you, girl!" Stephan laughed. "What is it gonna hurt to read the letter? Anyway, I'm off my dear. You call me whenever, no matter the time, ok?" he said as he got into his car and rolled down the window.

"Yes...ok."

"I love you, sweetie." He started the ignition.

"I love you too, Grandpa, and thank you, thank you for everything."

She stood there in the brisk air watching him drive off into the distance. She didn't move until the car disappeared around the corner. Then, with curiosity and anticipation, she opened the envelope. She took out the piece of paper and began to unfold it when a hundred dollar bill flew out onto the ground. Picking up the money, she folded it and stuffed it into her pocket. She straightened out the paper so she could read the letter.

"*Dear sweet babygirl,*

Wow, this day is finally here! My baby is in college and to be a lawyer at that! I always knew that you were going to make something of yourself. You have your father's brains and will to overcome obstacles. I want you to know that I am the happiest mother in the world. I remember back when you were born. Your father and I never told you, but you almost didn't make it. The umbilical cord was wrapped all around your little neck. Every second during delivery counted, because you were suffocating. Your grandpa, father, and even people from church came to pray for your safe arrival. God put His hands upon you and you made it without any defects or injuries. And you know what, God still has His hand on you, so trust Him. I know you have trust issues right now but He won't let you down. I finally understand why your dad had that scripture engraved into that necklace he gave you.

You are that tree, Willow. God has preserved you through all the adversity and your leaves are still green. Plant your trust in Him, sweetheart, and let your fruit come forth.

I know that I missed out on a lot when you were growing up. I wasn't there for you to protect you and to teach you the simple things of being a woman. I can't undo the past, all I can do is be better now and so enclosed is some money for you to use however you want. I am here for you and when you are ready Joseph and I would love to come and visit you. He misses you so much. He is always calling out his big sister's name, "Wilwo." That's pretty good to me for a two-year-old. Anyway, have fun, but not too much fun! I love you honey.

Love,

Mom

Willow wiped tears from her face. She refused to give in and hardened her heart. Heading back towards her dorm, she balled up the letter in a tight fist. She threw it into a nearby trash can as she entered her new home.

Walking into her room she found Megan dancing around with her music blasting through the speakers connected to her iPod. Megan was an interesting type of girl. She had her own style and flare, sporting a short haircut with one side shaved extremely low. There were strips of purple and blue running throughout her hair and she wore one long feather earring in her right ear and a small hoop in the other. But to

Willow's surprise, the girl could dress. Her style was very innovative and chic. Her makeup was on point too, with purple eyeshadow framing her slanted eyes that showed her Asian heritage. The features of Megan's face were so distinct, like a fashion model. Willow wondered if she had ever been in front of the camera, for she had the beauty and features for it.

She noticed that Megan had already begun to give her side of the room an artistic flare with two lava lamps and decorative abstract art pieces hanging up on the wall. Megan was so cool and fun; it made Willow for a brief moment think about becoming an art major like her, but that ended quickly because she had no type of artistic ability whatsoever.

Megan continued dancing and twirled around. She jumped at the sight of Willow. They both laughed hysterically and Megan ran to turn the music down.

"Oh, I'm sorry. I didn't hear you come in. I was in my own little world."

"It's ok, really, I don't mind. I really like how you're beefing your side of the room up. I feel inspired."

"Yeah, I have to. As you can see I'm no plain Jane. Sorry if it's too much."

They both giggled. "No not at all. Do you! I like it!" Willow replied.

"So you ready to have fun?! I heard there was some type of party going on back at the student union. We can finish unpacking later. You wanna go?" Megan asked. "Sure, let's go," Willow exclaimed.

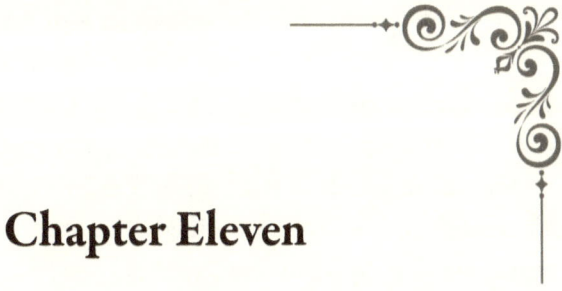

Chapter Eleven

It took a while for Willow to settle into her new life on campus as well as her work load. She had to maintain a 3.0 GPA to keep the full scholarship that she had and she stressed about it nonstop. She took all of the advice that was given her and she got to know each one of her professors and had a great relationship with her counselor. She constantly asked questions and was always found in the library. Sometimes she would end up staying overnight. It took her until her sophomore year to become relaxed and adjusted to the environment. Megan become a very good friend to her and they decided to continue to being roommates their second year. This time, they would be renting a student apartment together.

Then problems began to arise. Willow loved Megan and could talk to her about anything, but Megan was a social butterfly that loved to party. She would have parties and gatherings late at night during Willow's study time. Often times Willow got jealous of her to the point of anger because it seemed as though she never had any work to do, unless she was creating some type of art piece. She never studied; she just floated on by with ease, without a care, while Willow struggled for every A she got.

Pouring her heart into learning her material and preparing for exams didn't matter, because she still found herself in the danger zone in one of her government classes. If she didn't drop the class, she would have a failing grade on her record and lose her scholarship. There was no way she would be able to continue school without it. So her only option was to go through the long process of dropping the course. The worst part about it was she had to go to her department chair and get his signature to authorize the drop. She felt so embarrassed; she didn't want to have to go to him for something like this.

She sat nervously in the waiting area in the front of Dr. Morrison's office while his secretary notified him that he had a visitor. "Ms. Thompson, Dr. Morrison will see you now," she stated as she walked out of his office and returned to the seat behind her desk.

"Ok, thank you," Willow responded, walking into his office. Once inside, she was greeted by Dr. Morrison's picture-perfect smile that brightened the whole room. "Why hello, Ms. Thompson, close the door behind you and have a seat," he welcomed her while sitting behind his desk. He gestured with his hand towards one of the empty seats positioned in front of his desk. Willow got nervously quiet. She had almost forgotten how attractive he was. She was afraid she might choke on her words and say something stupid. She walked to the chair and sat down, holding her head slightly down.

"Are you ok?" he asked, sounding very concerned.

"Yes, I'm ok," she said, looking up with a forced smiled.

"Now there we go, wow what a pretty smile! So what brings you in here today?"

"Well I-I...a... am to say that I... I mean I'm having trouble in one of my classes and am afraid that I need to drop it."

"Oh really? You do know that the more you drop courses the more you get behind. Did you try to get tutored for it? Because we have some great tutors in the department?"

"Ummm....no, it is kind of too late for that. If I don't drop it now the failing grade will go on my cumulative record and drop my GPA."

"In other words, you will lose your scholarship. Yes, Ms. Thompson, I have looked at your file and I know that you are a bright student."

Willow saw the disappointment in his eyes and dropped her head again.

"Look, don't be so hard on yourself. This happens more than you think. You can jump back from this easily," he said optimistically.

"Thank you for the encouragement," Willow said as she handed him the form to sign to authorize the drop.

"Oh, no problem, beautiful!"

Did he just call me beautiful? Willow thought as she started blushing.

"Remember, I'm here for you. Anything you need let me know. Is there anything else I can do for you?"

"Uh, um, uh, no I think that's it. Thanks so much," she said getting up out of her chair.

He got up and walked with her slowly to the door. He handed her the form but didn't let go.

"Are you sure you don't need anything else from me?" He locked his eyes with hers and she was speechless. She was caught off guard by the sudden shift in his behavior.

"You know, I can make it so you never have to worry about losing your scholarship ever again, or any other bad grade for that matter." His demeanor had completely changed, no longer holding a professional composure, testing her as he came closer to her ear. "It only depends on how much you want it," he whispered, gently brushing her ear with his lips. Willow got lost in the moment and closed her eyes, completely captivated.

Then the door knob began to fidget and he swiftly stepped away from her. Willow was now free of his seduction. His secretary peeked her head in the doorway. "Sorry to interrupt, Dr. Morrison, but you have an important phone call on line one."

"Ok, but next time use the intercom, Jessica, thank you," he said in an irritated tone.

"Sure Dr. Morrison," Jessica said and looked at Willow.

"Are you okay darling? You look like you saw a ghost!"

"Oh, ye...yes I'm fine." Jessica left and closed the door and Willow began to power walk towards the door.

"Hey wait, you're forgetting something?" He picked up her form that had fallen to the floor when they were startled by the interruption. He extended it out to her and she went to grab the paper, but he yanked it away. She tried to grab it again and he yanked it away once more.

"Give it to me, please," she said nervously.

"I will, on one condition. You have to promise to come back and see me again real soon." Willow was uncomfortable and wanted to get out of there as fast as she could, especially after she got a good glimpse of his wedding ring shining in the light.

"Ok," she blurted.

"You promise? Say you promise," he taunted.

"I promise," she said, grabbing the paper and nearly sprinting out of the door.

Willow wanted to tell Megan or even the friends she had made in her study group of how Dr. Morrison had come on to her. But who was she kidding? No one would believe her. She barely believed it herself and it had happened to her. The scene kept replaying in her head, creating a mixture of emotions stirring within her. She was flattered that of all the girls on campus he came on to her. But he was a married man and probably had children. One thing was for sure. she was not going back to his office again, at least not by herself.

ONE NIGHT WILLOW AND her friend Doug stayed up late in the computer lab of the political science building studying for an exam. "I am beat, Willow. I think it is time for me to take it in. Look around, we are the only ones still here and the coach has put me on curfew for the game tomorrow. I am gonna get in trouble messing with you. Girl, you go hard with studying, I don't know if I can hang," Doug joked.

"Alright, I guess we can stop. Some sleep will do us some good." They both laughed and joked as they packed up their things.

Walking towards the main exit of the building, someone shouted from behind. "Ah, Ms. Thompson, I am glad I caught you. Can I see you for a minute please? I would like to discuss something with you." Willow's heart dropped; it was Dr. Morrison. They turned around and both said hello to him. "Sorry, but can it wait until the morning? It is kind of late and I have an exam tomorrow," she said quickly while backing towards the door. "No, ma'am, it's very important and it will not take that long. It is about that class you dropped. Come follow me up to my office," he demanded, not taking no for an answer.

She turned to Doug, "Will you go with me please?!"

With a regretful look in his eyes he said, "I can't, I am already late for curfew. If I don't go right now coach will bench me. I'm sorry. I gotta go." He began to run out the door and yelled, "I will see you tomorrow."

"Come on, Ms. Thompson, we don't have all night," Dr. Morrison yelled. Willow slowly followed him, dreading every step forward. *How could Doug just leave me hanging like that,* she thought. *Ok, I'll go up for a minute but keep my distance and the door open,* she reasoned with herself, seeing no way out. He was standing waiting for the elevator to come. She reached him right when the doors glided opened. She followed him inside and quickly moved into the far corner of the elevator. She was pushed up against the wall trying to get as much distance between them as she could. He looked over and smiled, "You don't have to be afraid. I just want to talk to you about improving your performance. That's all."

"We could have done that in the morning."

"Yes, you're right. But I wasn't sure you would come back. You haven't exactly been one to keep your word, now have you?"

Willow began to relax and let down her guard a bit. Maybe she was making too much of what had happened before. When they reached the top floor, they both walked in silence to his office area. Willow noticed that the front desk to the waiting room was vacant. Jessica, his secretary, had already gone home for the day. As they walked through his office doors, she became increasingly nervous again; he went to close the door behind them. "Wait! No, leave that open," Willow gestured to the door. He held his hands up as a sign of innocence and left the door open.

"Ok, have a seat."

"I prefer to stand."

"Ok, suit yourself. Are you adjusting well to your major?"

"I think I am doing well."

"I have been thinking about your performance and I wonder... uh.... do you think political science is right for you? You know this is a field where you may have to compromise your beliefs or values for the common good, or heck to get anywhere in the industry. How far are you willing to go?"

He stared up at her from behind his desk. She was mesmerized by his whole demeanor. He was so strikingly handsome.

"I... I don't know. I just want to help people who are in trouble. That is my main goal."

He sat silently staring at her for a minute, which was like a century to Willow.

"Ok, here are some of the things you can do to help you study more effectively for your government classes."

He stood up and picked up a little packet of papers from his desk and handed them to her. She took the papers and said, "That's it? Is this all you wanted to give me?"

He approached her and got in her personal space. "No, ma'am. Your suspicion is right. I just wanted to get you alone." He kept walking closer to her and she backed away with every step until she bumped into a nearby wall. "Why haven't you been back to see me?"

"I have been busy. You know, trying to stay on top of my grades," Willow said softly. He brushed his body up against hers. "You're making me uncomfortable, please move. I am ready to go. Plus I don't think your wife will appreciate you doing this," she said as she tried to squeeze between him and the wall to gain a clear path to the door. He slammed his arm up against the wall to trap her within the confined space. Then he moved closer stroking her face with his hand.

"What she doesn't know won't kill her. What's wrong Willow? I can take care of you. I can make sure you never have to worry about anything while you are here again. Just let me take care of you, baby."

He made his move and pressed his lips against hers and kissed her deeply. She abandoned her protest and gave in to the kiss as his hand moved from her face down to her hip. He wrapped his arms around her waist and cradled her body closer to his. Their kisses became longer and deeper and his hands took on a mind of their own, exploring her body. Suddenly Willow began to push him away as if she were waking from a deep sleep. "No, I can't do this! Move please," Willow pleaded. He pressed himself up against her harder, which made her fight back harder. He finally got tired of her pushing him away. He grabbed her arms and pinned them to the wall above her head. "Don't fight it, you want me just as much as I want you." Then he started kissing her neck while unbuttoning her blouse.

A FRAIL, SHORT GREY figure with a huge hump in its back stood beside Dr. Morrison, hunched over. It paid close attention to their every movement, watching in excitement, hoping from one foot to the next. Half of its face was deformed with dents and craters and it had no mouth. Lust had the upper hand and he made sure to have seducing spirits with him, swarming around to ensure his victory. They had complete charge of the room.

Petundan watched on pins and needles from his post as Lust took advantage of Willow. He wanted to protect her so badly, but he couldn't. God had commanded that there be no divine intervention for her in this season of her life. It was time for her to show God how much she depended on His will and not her own. "Come on, Willow, you have to make the right decision! Get out of your carnal mind! You must resist the lust of your flesh! This is a test. It's only a test! You know the right thing to do, please," Petundan cried.

WILLOW WAS GASPING for every breath nervously as he continued kissing and undressing her. She stopped fighting and decided to allowed him to have his way with her. She did want him and she wanted him bad. He had broken her down and at that moment she didn't care about the consequences of her actions. All she knew was that this moment felt good to her and she wasn't going to let it pass her by. Ignoring all of the convicting thoughts in her head, she focused on the fact that she couldn't believe that someone like him was interested in her, and the thought of not having to worry about her grades didn't hurt either. She had come to grips with the fact that she would hate herself in the morning, but for the moment she took the bait and gave herself to him right there in his office.

The next day Willow woke up to a knock at her bedroom door. She popped her head up and tossed wildly through the covers to sit up. She had almost forgotten where she was. She abruptly looked over at her alarm clock that said 11:00. "Oh no! I missed my 9:00," she yelled banging her hands down on the bed. Megan slowly opened the door, peeking in. "Good morning, sleepy head! What happened to you? You look like you got ran over last night," she laughed. Willow probably did look bad, because when she got home after her encounter with Dr. Morrison she cried to the wee hours of the morning until she fell asleep. "Any who, look what was just delivered to you this morning!"

Megan pulled out a glass vase holding a beautiful arrangement of red and yellow roses with a card and a small box from behind her back. Willow jumped out of bed and eagerly grabbed her present. "You and your boyfriend are so cute; you guys give me hope to one day find love. Hurry! Open it; I want to see what it is," Megan said cheerfully with a big smile of approval.

Willow became still for a moment. She had completely forgotten about Louis. It had slipped her mind that Valentine's Day was next week. They had already planned for him to come up so they could celebrate it together. How could she betray him so easily? They had planned to save themselves for their wedding night and she had broken that vow. Her self-worth spiraled down the more she thought about the trouble she had created. She made the decision right then that she had to break up with Louis. It wasn't fair to him that she cheated. She wanted to come completely clean and tell him everything, but that wouldn't be good considering that she had slept with the chairperson of her department. She couldn't bring herself to tell him. She couldn't bring herself to tell anyone, for that matter. Opening the envelope, she thought how sweet it was for Louis to send his present so early. It made her feel even worse. Willow started to read the card aloud.

"I enjoyed our time together last ni...."

Willow quickly stopped reading. "What? You were with Louis last night? Wow, I didn't know he was here already," Megan exclaimed. "I can't wait to meet him finally!"

Willow cleverly thought of an excuse to hide her transgression. "Ummm....no, no he's not here yet. I think he's just talking about our conversation we had over Skype. We stayed on there for hours last night."

"Oh oookay," Megan said, still pondering what Willow had just told her, not sure if she believed it or not. Before Megan could ask more questions Willow got up and began to push her out towards the door. "Look, this is kind of private. I think I want to read this alone. I will come out and show you the present when I get done, ok, bye!" Willow pushed Megan out to the hallway and then slammed the door in her face.

"OK! Well you don't have to do me like that. Dang, girl, you almost made me cuss. Just for that you're not getting any of the breakfast I just made, and it's good too!!" Megan yelled from behind the closed door, feeling a little rejected. Willow ignored Megan, captivated by the note. She sat back on the bed and continued to read.

I hope that we can spend more nights like that in the future.
Please have dinner with me tonight. Don't worry, no one will find us.
Yours truly,
You know who

As Willow read the card a chill ran down her spine. She hadn't thought that he would want to see her again, and so soon. She reminisced on her night with him and then she snapped back to reality. She opened the little box. Inside were a pair of sparkling diamond earrings. She gasped at the sight of them and yelled out in pleasure. "Wow!" She immediately put them on and sashayed in the mirror, gawking at herself, no longer feeling condemned, but hopeful for the future of this exciting new relationship. Twirling around, she gave no acknowledgement to the fact that he was a married man and neither did she acknowledge God in the matter, who was watching the whole time.

The phone rang over and over again. "Come on, Louis, pick up the phone," Willow said to herself.

"Hello. Hey, Willow!"

"Hey, how you doin'?"

"I'm better now that you've called. I can't wait to come and see you tomorrow. I miss you so much, babe."

"Look, Louis, let me get straight to it. I don't think that's a good idea."

"What...we..."

"I know we had planned for you to come visit me this weekend, but I have been thinking, and I don't think this long distance thing is gonna work."

"What are you talking about?"

"I mean, we hardly ever talk or see each other. I don't like this."

"But I thought we were doing good."

"We were...I mean we are... I mean I just think we need to be friends, okay?"

"Wait, hold up," Louis took a long pause. "This is coming out of nowhere. Don't blame this on the long-distance. You found someone else, didn't you?"

"What!? No, that's not it," Willow lied.

"Come on Willow, I'm not stupid. I know what it is. At least have enough dignity to tell me the truth. No! You know what, don't even worry about it. Go ahead and do yo' thang. Have your fun. At least you could have spared me until after Valentines! What's up with you, Willow? I've never known you to be a liar. Just tell the truth."

"Wait. Louis, I'm sorry. You're right. There is someone else." Willow gave up on the lie.

"Okay, 'ight baby girl. Just know that he ain't gonna love you like I do. Remember that." Louis hung up the phone.

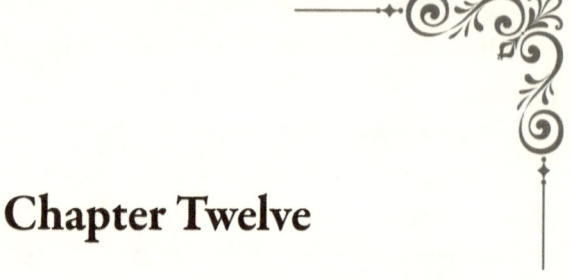

Chapter Twelve

Willow became a girl that lived a double life. Driven college student by day and mysterious mistress by night. Although she didn't see herself as a mistress at all, because she never had to deal with his wife and he never spoke of her. He didn't even wear his ring when they were together. She dove head first into the relationship with no hesitation. She wanted to forget about how she had lied to and hurt Louis. She thought the more time she invested into Daniel the more easily she would be able to hide from her selfishness. Their relationship had grown so much that she honestly believed that he loved her and that they would one day be together. They saw each other routinely for about three months and they were not missing a beat. He had told her to call him by his first name, Daniel, when they were alone. He also spoiled her with gifts, weekends dat nights, and a spring break vacation she had only dreamed about. He kept his promise about her grades and she took advantage of that by not going to class whenever she didn't feel like it. All of this had to count for something, 'cause in her mind she was the one and only. Until the day things drastically changed and the truth hit her right in the face.

In passing weeks Daniel all of a sudden started to distance himself from her little by little. Missing her phone calls and not calling back. He stood her up a couple of times when they were supposed to go on a date or meet up. She was tired of getting his voicemail or numerous excuses as to why they couldn't see each other. When they spent time together, they had talked and laughed before, but things turned to him always finding some reason to be agitated with her. The trips stopped, but he still wanted the midnight rendezvous whenever he had the urge. This left Willow questioning where she stood with him and where things had gone wrong.

"Willow, Willow! Wake up! You are going to be late for your exam!" Megan yelled as she pounded on her bedroom door. Willow sluggishly sat up in bed, feeling groggy from a wild night's sleep. "Okay! I'm—..." She smacked her hands up to her mouth unable to complete her comment. She jumped up and sprinted to her bathroom and hovered her head over the toilet, expelling everything that was in her stomach. Megan heard what was going on from the other side of the door and barged into the room. "Are you alright?" she asked as she ran into the bathroom to help hold Willow's hair back. Willow continued to vomit and Megan comforted her by patting her on the back.

When Willow came up for air Megan handed her a towel to wipe her mouth.

"I'm ok now," Willow said out of breath. "This must be some kind of bug 'cause I haven't been feelin' right all week."

"What do you mean you haven't been feelin' *right?*"

"Well, I'm nauseous all the time and I'll get light headed sometimes for no apparent reason. Headaches come and go like clockwork."

"Ummm, when was the last time you had, you know, your period?"

Willow sat on the bathroom floor in silence as she looked up a Megan, who was leaning on the bathroom sink.

"Uhh, I don't know... I DON'T KNOW!! Oh my goodness I don't know!" She panicked as she got up and ran to the sink to wash her mouth out. Megan moved out of her way and muttered, "It could be." When Willow was finished, she ran to the bedroom. "This can't be. Lord please don't let this be," she screamed. She threw on some clothes and asked Megan to take her to the drug store to get some home pregnancy tests.

The next morning Willow walked into Daniel's office and approached the front desk where his secretary was sitting manicuring her nails and humming to the music playing in the background. "Hey, I need to see Dr. Morrison please," Willow said calmly. Jessica looked up at her and then rolled her eyes, "Ugh, ok, have a seat over there and I will let him know that you are here." Willow sat down, wondering why she had caught an attitude with her. Jessica picked up the phone and notified Daniel that Willow was there. She hung up the phone and said, "He told me to let you know that he is in a meeting right now and you should schedule another time to come in next week." Willow's heart dropped as she got up to leave. "Do you want to schedule a time?" Jessica asked in a little giggle. "No, that's okay," Willow said holding back her tears.

She slowly walked out of the office into the hallway. Anger grew with every step she took until she made up her mind that she was going to demand to see him. She marched back into the waiting area of the office and noticed that Jessica was no longer at her desk. She passed on by the reception desk, straight to Daniel's office door, opening it with great force. She inhaled with shock as she entered the room.

"What in the world is going on in here?!" Willow shouted. To her dismay, Jessica was sitting on Daniel's lap with his shirt opened and her blouse half way off.

Willow got the answer to her question as to why things had changed between Daniel and her. She had become old news to him, he had moved on. They both jumped up and Jessica clumsily fixed her clothes. Embarrassed, Willow hurried out and shut the door behind her. Then she stopped and barged back in.

"What is this!? How could you?" she screamed at the top of her lungs. Jessica got up in Willow's face, "What's this? The little baby gonna cry now? Oh please, he's my man now, honey. So get...."

"Jessica, leave us for a minute. I want to talk to her alone," Daniel interrupted. Jessica got quiet and walked out the door, bumping into

Willow's shoulder as she passed by. Willow resisted the urge to yank Jessica by her weave and drag her up and down the hallway.

"I am sorry about what you saw, but you entered at your own risk. You were told to come back next week," he said nonchalantly. Willow took a few steps into the room.

"You're a fake. This whole time you were playin' me. Is that what you do, huh? Go around seducing innocent women into giving you what you want?! What about your wife?" she continued to yelled in anger.

"Oh don't you give me that. You didn't care about my wife when you thought it was all about you! Keep my wife out of your mouth. She is none of your concern!"

"But, what about me? What about us?"

"What about us? Come on, Willow, you know the game. You played your part real well. I'll give you that. But we are coming to the end of the year. It's time to get back to reality. Maybe we can pick this back up next semester, you know, if I feel like it."

Willow's world was falling apart and she didn't know what to do. She went up to one of the chairs in front of his desk and sat down.

"Oh yeah, I played my part *REAL* good, huh?!"

"Yeah, but falling in love was never in the cards, baby."

"Well, I guess I'm not the only one who played their part good 'cause, uh.... You're going to be a father." Willow threw a pregnancy test on his desk as the evidence.

"I already got two beautiful children at home. I don't know what you talkin' 'bout."

"I'm pregnant with your baby!"

"What?! Please Willow! You're not gonna get me with that one. You and I both know that you are not pregnant and if you are it sho' ain't mine! I got it from you easy. There's no tellin' who else you been givin' it up to. What you tryin' to do, trap me!? Or better yet break up my home?"

"WHAT!? Are you really going to treat me like this right now? You are a grown man acting like a boy!"

"Whatever, look, do I have to spell it out for you? It is over! O-V-E-R, over! So I need you to get over it and get out my office, ASAP!"

"So it's over just like that? What am I supposed to do?"

"I don't know. I suggest you get rid of it. Or find out who the daddy really is. I don't care. Just get out NOW!"

Willow rushed out of his office in tears. She had imagined things going the complete opposite of what just happened. She had been so naive believing that he had real feelings for her. She realized she was just a toy he had used for his own enjoyment. What was she going to do now? He would never claim her baby, and being a single mother was not how she had pictured her life. She was sure she would have to fight in court for any type of help from him. Her life was ruined as far as she was concerned. She could kiss her scholarship goodbye for sure if she didn't pass her finals, and she hadn't been going to class or doing any of her work. Passing her finals would be nearly impossible for her to do. She was so ashamed she slumped over in regret as she walked home.

Willow stayed up all night with Megan, crying her eyes out. She told her what had happened, making sure not to leave out one detail. Megan was outraged, pacing back and forth. "I can't believe that jerk! I knew he was bad news; any man as smooth as that has got to be bad news! You mean to tell me he had the nerve to say "it" wasn't his? That's crazy! And you! What in the world were you thinking messing with a married man and the department chair?! You have got to tell someone so that he can lose his job. If you don't report him I will!

NO! Megan, you can't. Don't do that. I will be humiliated all across campus. Promise me you won't do that.

This isn't right Willow. I bet he preys on students all the time. This is just not right! Why didn't you tell me what was going on? We are friends, aren't we? You do know I am here for you right?!"

Willow was lounged back on the couch, drained from crying. "Yes I know Meg, I was just too ashamed and I knew it was wrong the whole time." She stopped to blow her nose, "What am I gonna do now? I can't keep the baby. I don't know how to be a mother."

"You can do it, Willow, and I'm sure your grandpa and mom would help you."

"I don't want to put that burden on them, and how will they see me after this? I don't want to disappoint my grandpa. How can I tell him that I'm pregnant by a married man? And what about school? No, I can't do it."

"It will work out! Don't make a hasty decision that you will regret later."

"I can't possibly have that dog's baby. What will I tell the baby when it gets older and ask about their father? This is too much, I can't!"

"Willow, you just take it one step at a time. You can handle that when the time comes. Look, just think about it a little more, ok? Promise me."

"Ok. I will."

Weeks passed and Willow had made up her mind that she was going to abort the baby. She didn't tell Megan about her plans for fear of her trying to talk her out of it, or worse yet her being judged by her friend. That morning Willow called the only person she had left to call on, her study partner Doug. He wasn't just a study partner but he was one of her good friends that she had meet in her class upon arriving to Chapel Hill. And he had always been kind to her and she felt comfortable enough to ask him for help. She told Doug a very limited amount of her story, making sure to leave out who the father was. She asked him if he would go with her to the appointment that was planned for the next day. He agreed and offered to help in any other way he could.

After her appointment Doug dropped her off at home. Willow rushed into her apartment in an oversize sweat suit, stumbling by

Megan in the kitchen, and went straight to her room without acknowledging her presence. She crawled into bed moaning out in pain and curled up in the covers. Megan entered her room. "You did it, didn't you?" Willow used all the energy she could muster and said yes softly. Her friend went around to the side of the bed where she was curled and sat beside her. She rubbed her back. "I am here for you. I would have like to have been there with you for support. You should have told me. But what's done is done. Are you ok?" Willow was so grateful for her caring friend. "No, but I will be. It was horrible and I am in so much pain."

For the next few weeks Willow isolated herself from the outside world. Megan had to beg her to come out of her room or even to eat. She slept all day and all night. It was no surprise to her when she saw her grades at the end of the semester. There was a pattern of D's and F's all in a row with one C. But she had a 1.20 GPA and in her mind, it should have been lower than that. When she received the pink letter letting her know she was on academic probation and that her scholarship was no longer active she immediately started the process to drop out of school.

She had to decide what she was going to do. She wanted to go back and stay with her grandfather, but she didn't want to call him because she was too ashamed. Megan basically begged her to continue to be her roommate and for her to just get a job in town. But Willow gently declined the idea because she wanted to be a far away from Daniel as possible. She felt like being back at home would help her clear her mind from all the drama and disappointment. It appeared as though she only had one other option. After days of deep contemplation she mustered up the courage to call her mother.

Chapter Thirteen

"Hello?" Tammie answered the phone.

"Hey momma."

"Willow is that you?"

"Yes."

"What's wrong honey? You sound like you've been crying."

Willow sobbed loudly, unable to respond to her mother. She hated that she had to confide in her mom but she didn't know what else to do.

"Willow, what is it. What's wrong?"

"I don't want to be here anymore. Can I come stay with you?"

"Willow! Well this is a surprise. You're just gonna up and leave school just like that? I thought that everything was going pretty good. Maybe you are just homesick."

"Mom, this just isn't for me. I lost my scholarship and I am on academic probation. Please let me come stay with you."

"Wait a minute Willow..." Tammie was about to start an argument with Willow, but caught herself. After the strain that she caused on their fragile relationship she did not want to do anymore harm by lecturing her. "Ok, baby, if that's what you want. My door is always open to you. Does your grandpa know that you're leaving school?"

"No." Willow busted out crying again with just the thought of telling him she was dropping out.

"Oh sweetie, I am coming to get you right now. It's gonna be okay."

She went home with her mother and told herself that she would get her life together. She couldn't believe that she had given in to a married man and murdered her own child. She longed for her child so much that she had recurring dreams of the baby. Oh how she longed to hug and kiss her baby and to make things right. She prayed to God, something she rarely did those days, repeatedly asking for forgiveness. But it didn't matter because nothing could take away the sadness and heaviness that had entered her heart.

The truth was God forgave her right when she asked, but she was the one who didn't forgive herself. God was more of a fairy tale to her these days due to the many adversities she had experienced. She was angry with herself and God and so she dug herself into a deep, dark, ditch.

WILLOW FELT SO EXPOSED, so naked. All of her misfortunes and failures played out right in front of her. "So I am facing the ugliness. How is this supposed to help me?" Willow questioned Dregus with no resolve.

"Oh, I'm sorry. I didn't make this clear. None of this is going to change anything. The outcome of your actions are sealed. There's really nothing you can do. YOU are here because you were careless with your life. Even when you were alive you lived like you were dead! You even had others around you try to help direct you in the right path and what did you do? You completely ignored them to your own destruction. I wanted you to see that there were things going on all around you that were bigger than you, that were invisible to you. My task is to show you what lead you here so maybe you can come to grips with your fate! The reality is that God wants nothing to do with you. You have disgraced Him and he knows you not!" Dregus yelled with rage.

Willow shivered with fear and covered her ears with her hands. The harmonious melody that was usually heard when he spoke turned into a clutter of clashing cords, hurting her ears. He walked over to her and held out his hand, holding the last accuser.

"You have revisited your past; now it's time for you to face your future. Here, take the accuser and toss it into the water so that it may show you what is to be, for this is the path you have chosen."

Feeling the pressure and afraid of what would happen if she didn't, she took the pebble and threw it into the river. It plopped in the water and nothing happened. After a few seconds the water morphed into a river of blood. Fish that were once swimming happily now floated to the surface, dead. The blood shifted to a hot, fiery, golden red lava stream consuming all in its path. Willow started shaking her head and stepping back. She looked around earnestly in search for Dregus.

"Dregus! Dregus! Where are you?!" she screamed but he had disappeared into thin air.

Gliding up from the lava with a victor's stance came a knight with dark armor. He wore no helmet, so she was able to get a good look of his face. His head was a skull with burning flesh peeling off and his eye sockets glowed with golden flames and two sharp horns on the top of his head. Suspended in air, with lava dripping from his armor, he raised his right arm and spun around the spiked ball and chain that was in his hand. Willow turned to run in horror as the chain was flung in her direction.

It wrapped around both of her ankles and forced her to the ground face forward. Screaming and scrapping at the ground with her fingers for any kind of leverage, the malicious aggressor pulled her towards the river. As he pulled her closer to the river, hands covered in red slime and distorted faces of morbid anguish protruded from the boiling lava. They were making the most horrendous groans and screams that Willow had ever heard. She could feel their pain with every groan. The hands reached for her as her feet came closer to the riverbank with the intent of pulling her into their misery. She squirmed, lifting her feet to dodge their grasp in a panic, causing herself to flip over on her back.

One of the deformed figures climbed waist high out of the lake of fire and grabbed her wrist. At the its mere touch Willow heard sizzling and yelled in agony, yanking her arm out of its grip with all of her might. She looked down at her wrist and saw the glowing mark in the shape of a hand that was printed on her. The knight looked down at her and shook with a rambunctious laugh, exposing his blood sucking fangs.

"Jesus, help me please! Please give me another chance!" she screamed with her eyes sealed shut. "Stop! It is not time yet!" Willow opened her eyes when she heard Dregus' voice. The Knight and the horrid faces in the river froze in place like statues. Dregus walked up to Willow who was still lying on the ground, legs bound and all. He waved his hand and all of her attackers and the chain around her ankles disappeared and everything was miraculously back to normal.

Did that just really happen? Willow could not even comprehend what she had just experienced. She laid on the ground flat as a board, afraid to move the slightest inch. In a trance of unbelief, she finally came to herself when she realized that Dregus was walking away from her to cross the nearby bridge that she had noticed before. "Wait! Wait for me!" she jumped up, holding her wrist from where she had been burned. She looked at her wound to assess the damage and saw that the hand print had turned into a blackened scar.

"Dregus! Dregus! Hold on, don't leave me!" she shouted in an uneven tone. He kept walking, bluntly ignoring her request in a daunting silence. Close by in the distance she heard squawking noises and something brushing through the bushes. Jumping in fear she turned all around back and forth looking in every direction. She was so on edge from the horrible event that had just taken place that her hearing had been sharpened. She was sensitive to every sound, no matter whether great or small, and they all gave her goosebumps.

A squirrel ran across the grass and up a tree, making her scream out in horror. She sprinted to the bridge and hurried to catch up with Dregus. "Hey!! Don't you hear me?" she screamed. By that time, he was in front of the beautiful archway that she had admired earlier. Willow watched as he bowed his head and whispered something and then proceeded to walk forward, but when he walked through the opening turned into a black swirl as it swallowed him up.

She almost lost her balance as she watched in amazement of the hidden portal. Her run turned to a nervous walk. She finally got up to the magical archway and stood in front of it. She looked through with widened eyes and her lungs void of air, because for the moment she had forgotten how to breathe. One part of the mystery to the portal was revealed when she got close enough to investigate. It appeared that the arch was really a mirror of some sort. But the image that faced her through the looking glass was nothing like what she remembered of herself. The image paralleled her movements, but it was highly distorted and offensively ugly.

Her hands were where her ears were supposed to be and her right arm was where her right leg was normally and vice versa. Her head and torso had switched places, and her face was deformed. One side bubbled out bigger than the other and her mouth was askew, with her eyes on her cheeks. Her chest was transparent and she could see a corroded black thing that mimicked a heart pumping up and down. It was cracked down the center, hanging together by a small piece of flesh.

Willow was freaked out and disgusted by the sight that was before her. She felt a panic attack drawing near. Closing her eyes, she tried to calm herself as tears ran down her face. She felt her knees began to weaken. "Come on, Willow, you can do this! Get it together girl! DON'T be afraid. You are NOT afraid!" she falsely motivated herself.

A strong cool wind came and danced through the leaves of the trees surrounding her. As she listened to the symphony of the breeze, she settled down as it blew across her face, drying away the water trails down her cheeks. It continued to blow around her and she felt comforted, like she was in a sweet embrace. She got so quiet and still she heard a small whisper that echoed within her.

"Be strong and of good courage; be not afraid, neither be thou dismayed: for the Lord thy God is with thee wherever thou go. You shall not look this way always. It is only a light affliction. I have ordered your steps; pass through, beloved." Willow opened her eyes with newfound strength and security. She looked into the mirror, but this time she was not shaken. She stood taller, with her knees now restored. Then she ran straight forward, letting the portal consume her, eager to meet the unknown.

Crossing over to the other side, she fell to the ground on another dirt path. She looked up to find Dregus standing before her with his arms crossed over his chest. Apparently, he had been waiting for her the whole time. "Hmmm, I didn't think that you would be able to do it," he said in surprise. He turned around and started to walk down the long winding path that led deeper into the forest. Willow looked around and surveyed her new surroundings.

They had to have entered a different dimension. The gorgeous vivid world of color was far behind her now. Here the sky was gloomy and overcast. It was weird how the scenery was all grey scaled like she was in an old black and white film. She steadily got off of the ground and began to pat the dirt off of her blue jeans. She abruptly came to a stop when she noticed that even she herself was without color. Her jeans were no longer blue, but a light grey, and her hands were a darker grey tone. She looked up from her new discovery. "But Dregus...." slipped out of her mouth. Dregus remained the same vibrant colors, unaffected by his surroundings.

She ran to catch up to him. "Hey, what did you mean back there? When you said you didn't think I would be able to do it." He looked over at her for a minute and huffed, showing a quick sign of annoyance.

"Usually, I have to come back and pull them through."

"Wait. What? You mean to tell me there have been others?"

"Oh yes! Many before you, child."

"Really? And you save them all from...from..."

"From Hell?" he said with a big grin on his face.

"Yeah, from Hell."

"Isn't there a bigger, more pressing question that you would like answered?"

Willow thought for a minute and then asked, "Well, what was that we just went through?"

"That is the window of truth and *YES,* that is how you really look. It removes all smokescreens and reveals what is truly there."

She dropped her head in disappointment. Hearing the truth, she could feel her heart tear a little more.

"Where are we going? Do I get to talk to Jesus now?" barely got out of her mouth in a frail tone. Dregus ignored her question as he walked ahead of her.

"Where is God? Doesn't he want to see me?!" Willow called out again attempting to get an answer from the weird creature.

"NO! Didn't I tell you before? He has no desire to see you! The window of truth showed you how ugly you are. Now, what makes you think you can be in His presence!?" Dregus roared as he turned to face her.

Willow was taken back by his response, but she believed him. For how could God dare to even look at her in her current condition? Dregus turned back around and walked down the path. "But there is hope for you yet, child. Right now, you know in part and you see in part. In this land there is an uncommon tree that holds knowledge of the whole. If you partake of its fruit your eyes will be opened and you will know all. You will be as God and able to choose your own fate." His words and melodic voice seduced her ears. "I am taking you there now."

Her mind raced, thinking about all the power she would have with infinite knowledge, and how she would escape Hell and all of its torment. She hoped that he was telling the truth and allowed endless possibilities to race through her mind. Then there was a turning in the pit of her stomach. Her grandpa and pastor had never talked about any of this, and deep down she didn't feel right about what he'd said, but she ignored the feeling.

Chapter Fourteen

As Dregus continued talking, they passed by a small narrow opening in the forest off to the left of them. Willow stopped and turned curiously and peered inside. Beyond the opening there was a vast field of stale ground with small bushes spontaneously sprouting around. A narrow bumpy path went through the field, leading to the center, where a bare tree with thin branches rested. It bore no leaves and no fruit. The whole area was unappealing and looked like a drought. The field bore no sign of travelers passing through it. Dregus noticed Willow being distracted by the field. "Oh, don't worry about that dead, dry place. Come, your second chance awaits you just ahead," Dregus said, while pointing ahead to where the path merged into another clearing. She heard him, but for some reason she couldn't take her eyes off of the tree. Feeling compelled, she took a step forward to go through the opening. With great force Dregus grabbed her arm and yanked her back to the dirt road.

"Do you want this rare opportunity or not? You know, I could have allowed you to be taken to your doom, let's not forget! But *NO*, I am here offering you the chance of a new life! Don't be ungrateful!" he shouted uncontrollably.

"I know and I'm sorry. I was just looking. Goodness, don't pop a vein, ok?!" she said, yanking her arm from his strong claw. Willow didn't understand what the big issue was about her wanting to explore. "Okay, look..." Dregus said as he clasped his claws together. "I did not mean to yell. I just don't want you to make the wrong decision.

We both know that you have not been too good at making the right decisions in the past. So please, I beg of you, do not miss what I have to show you.

Willow looked back through the opening to the bare field and then back to Dregus. "Okay, I understand and you are right. I don't make the best decisions. Lead the way, I'm following you." They walked forward to the clearing ahead.

Like flicking on a light switch the color came flooding back into view as they stepped into the grassy meadow. It was a vivid green with a mixture of violets and dandelions scattered about. An abundance of dandelion seeds flew carelessly around in the air. As they walked, Willow saw that there was a path of bent grass that was created by many foot impressions of those who had come before her. Willow stopped in her tracks when she spotted the tree that Dregus has told her about. It was enormous. It had to be the biggest of all the tress she had seen thus far. Standing there with such beauty that beamed out on all of its surroundings. The clouds had opened up over the land and the sun shined down right on the tree like a spotlight displaying treasure. It produced plump gigantic fruit that peeked beyond the big green leaves. "Whoa! How beautiful!" she exclaimed.

Her mouth began to salivate as she saw the juicy fruit. She rubbed her stomach, which was growling in hunger, having no remembrance of its last meal. Dregus watched her from the corner of his eyes and smile with pleasure from her reaction. "Its beauty is nothing compared to its glory or the glory *YOU* will have after you taste its fruit," he said with his nose tilted in the air.

Even though the tree was wonderful, Willow couldn't help but think about the mysterious land holding the frail lonely tree. "Just out of curiosity, what is that place back there that we just passed?" she probed.

"It's a place of death. Trust me, you don't want to go in there. Bad things happen there," he warned.

"But *HERE,* dear child," he pointed to the bountiful tree, "you shall not die, but have life and live more *ABUNDANTLY!*" He smiled with excitement glistening in his eyes. That was the first time she had seen him so enthused, which excited her as well. "And just think after you eat, God will be ready to meet with you." Moments after he spoke, the whisper that had helped her go through the portal came to her once again saying, "the field of mustard seeds."

"Field of mustard seeds?" she said aloud to herself.

Dregus abruptly turned and squinted his eyes at her and his smile quickly went away. "How do you know that? What do you hear? You have the ears to hear, don't you?" He spoke slowly, inching closer to her. Willow didn't know all of the Bible, but she knew some scripture from reading on her own and from her grandpa. She remembered that the mustard seed was used in a parable that Jesus told the disciples when He was explaining to them the importance of faith and the kingdom of heaven. The place looked so dry and without substance though. And she knew that a seed can only grow in fertile soil so the name didn't match the area from what she could see. There was nothing there, surely nothing that could help her situation. But still, she wondered why Dregus had wanted to keep the name a secret and who was whispering answers in her ear. She was taken aback by Dregus' suspicion. *What was he hiding?* That was the only thing that made her curious about that place, but she wasn't going to let Dregus know that. Not knowing what to say she casually responded "I...I... don't know, lucky guess I suspect."

Dismissing her response, he continued. "You do have ears." He stepped back and turned away from her. "Ha, this should be fun; I love a good challenge," he mumbled to himself rubbing his hands together.

Dregus turned back around and examined her for a long while, making her uncomfortable. His voice switched from the tune of a piano, but now when he spoke it was that of harps and strings that serenaded her, putting her in a trance. "I thought you were hungry. That place has nothing to eat. Why wonder when there is plenty here, more than enough? Look at the beauty of this tree and all it has to offer you," he said, slowly moving towards the tree. She followed his every move and placed her eyes upon the magnificent tree. As she was drawn with seduction's force she began to feel foolish for even being concerned about the bare tree when a tree of abundance and opportunity was offered so freely to her.

"For I take the foolish things to confound the wise." The gentle whisper had come back, breaking up her thoughts. She stopped and listened in a very still posture. The symphony that was played from Dregus' mouth became muffled, as if there were a barrier between her and him. "Live by faith, not by sight. Don't be fooled by the things that you see with your natural eyes. For the things that are seen are temporal and the things that are unseen are eternal. Come to me all who are heavy laden, and I will give you rest. Eat from the bread of heaven and have eternal life."

Willow closed her eyes and absorbed the words that were spoken to her. After a moment of deafening silence, she opened her eyes and turned and looked back in the direction of the small opening that beckoned to her.

"Ummm, Dregus, this tree you have shown me is beautiful and... great but I think I am supposed to go back there to the other tree," she said, turning back to him who stood watching her every move. "Don't get me wrong, I really appreciate everything you've done for me and for bringing me here but I just don't feel that this is my way. Am I really supposed to have the power to choose my own fate? I am not my own judge?" Dregus stared at her for a moment in deep thought. Then his eyes shuffled left to right, slowly increasing in speed until all she could see where the whites of his eyes. "Dregus.... What's happening?!" she said backing away.

His body was twisting a contorting in every direction and his face started to stretch and bend while his hair turned black. It was no longer the long mane but a tamed low cut. His skin flashed through many different colors until it settled on a copper tone. The cracking of his bones was so loud that it echoed in the distance and lingered in the air and his giant structure compressed down to that of a six-foot frame. All of the hair that was on his body shed and dropped to the ground and a white T-shirt and jeans shorts formed, covering his otherwise bare body. His face was the last thing to change into that of a human man.

Willow watched from behind a bush that she had run to during the odd shapeshifting. The whole time she was silent, unable to make a sound. She stayed there, paralyzed, with her hand over her mouth and her eyes almost popping out of her head. Dregus' eyes, which were still totally white, rolled forward and shown forth light green, completing his metamorphoses. When she got a good look at his new appearance, she couldn't believe it. She jumped from her hiding place and yelled, "Louis! Wait, what? Louis? Dregus? Louis? Is it really you!?" She ran up to him and gave him a good looking over.

She looked at him suspiciously, keeping her distance. "Willow, it is me Louis," he said, holding his hands out towards her, asking for a hug.

"No, you're not. How could that be? You were just, just.... someone... something else. Where is Dregus?!" she said in horror.

"Listen to me, ok. I am Louis and I am here to help you. You must not make the wrong decision right now! This is your final test, Willow. You must block out that voice that you're hearing; it is a trick of the enemy, and he is deceiving you."

"Wait. Wait...wait. If you are here, then that means that you're.... dead, or being tested like I am?"

"Look, Willow, we don't have time for the specifics, but Dregus brought me through to help you make the right decision. I love you and I can't stand the thought of you suffering in Hell forever!"

She looked over at Louis in disbelief, but it sounded and looked exactly like him. The sight of him made her think about how good he was to her. He had stood by her when she got arrested and he even continued to love her and be there for her after she broke up with him to be with Daniel. She shook her head at the thought of Daniel. How could she have been so stupid. She had broken Louis' heart by telling him the truth of her new relationship. Even though she had tried to lie to him, she just couldn't. That was one thing about her, she always believed in telling the truth no matter what the consequences were. All the love she felt in her heart for Louis came rushing back to her in that very moment. Her mind drifted to the day he came to see her after she dropped out of school.

"WHAT IS GOING ON WITH you? You can talk to me." Louis was sitting in the love seat across the way, facing the couch that Willow was curled up on in her sweats. She stared out the window, too embarrassed to face him. Louis exhaled loudly, "Are you not even going to acknowledge me in any kind of way? I didn't just come from down the street you know. I drove over three hours to get here. Your mom let me know that you were staying with her and she told me you dropped out of school. She's really worried about you. Why haven't you returned any of my phone calls?" he asked with frustration. Willow shrugged roughly and continued to place her focus out the window as a means to hide her watery eyes. "Look at me Willow, please, talk to me. I'm worried about you. What's going on?" he shouted while standing up with his hands lifted in a demanding posture. Still there was no response from her.

Tammie angrily stepped into the living room. She had been listening and watching Louis desperately trying to reach her daughter.

"Willow Janelle Thompson, you get up from there right now! Are you really going to sit and ignore this boy after he's gone out of his way to come and see you? He's still in school ya know, the place where you should be! I can't believe you, young lady. You should be ashamed of yourself!

"ME!" Willow stomped up from the couch and pointed to her chest. "I'm the one who should be ashamed? Well, I'm not the only one! You should be ashamed! You are the one who treated me like trash! I HATE YOU!" Willow stormed out of the room and out the front door. Tammie gasped and covered her mouth in shock from the amount of disrespect. There was an awkward silence in the room until Louis broke it, "Don't worry I'll go and talk to her. Everything will be ok." He stood there for a minute and took Tammie's hand and squeezed it. Then he walked out the front door and found Willow on the front porch, balled up, still in a blank stare. He sat down beside her and rubbed her back. "Come with me, I want to take you somewhere," he said calmly. Now his demeanor was softened and of great concern. He stood up and reached his hand out towards her. His voice broke her gaze and she turned to him to find his hand opened towards her. She looked up at the handsome young man that stood above her. Looking into his sparkling brown eyes, she knew she didn't deserve to be in his presence.

Why won't he just move on, she thought. She deserved for him to never speak to her again. Thanks to her need to live on the edge and the selfishness that had been growing inside her, she had not only ruined her life but had also broken many hearts along the way. She went to put her slender hand in his and then hesitated, pulling back a little. He quickly took her hand in his with a secure grip. He bent down towards her and whispered in her ear, "I am not letting you go this time." She got warm and tingly all over. That was the first time that she felt alive since she had the abortion. Slowly getting up, she fell into his arms and gave him a heartfelt hug. "Whoa girl, you have wasted away! Have you been eating?!" he asked as he wrapped his arms around the tiny waist that her big sweat shirt concealed. Willow buried her face into his chest and cried uncontrollably. "Shhh...shhh. It's ok, please don't cry." Louis consoled her and rocked her in his arms.

Chapter Fifteen

After Willow calmed down they left to go to the special place Louis had planned for her. "Aww, Crystal Creek Park! We haven't been here in so long!" she said with excitement as they pull into a parking space. She smiled and turned to Louis and gave him a peck on the cheek. "Thank you for bringing me here." She felt a little like herself again, at least for that moment in time. Getting out of the car, Willow slammed the door in a rush and ran ahead of Louis racing to the nearby swings. This was a game they would always play upon their arrival. When Louis realized what was happening, he sprinted towards the swings in an effort to pick up the slack.

Willow laughed the whole way there. When she reached the swings, she turned around and jumped up and down. "I won! I won! Come on slow-poke!" She teased him while sticking out her tongue. She teased him with no mercy, because she had never won before. Louis came charging for her without slowing his pace. Running right up to her like a linebacker, he playfully picked her up on his shoulder and twirled her around. They both were laughing and she screamed, "Put me down!" over and over again until he lowered her on the ground and began to tickle her as she laid in the cool grass. She couldn't remember the last time she had laughed so hard, rolling around and gasping for air. She managed to get out, "Stop!" in a silent laugh. He finally stopped and dropped to the ground to lay beside her exhausted body.

They settled there for some time while both of their lungs went into over drive. "We did use to have such a good time together... didn't we?" Willow sighed in relaxation as she turned towards him. Their eyes met as if it were for the first time. Louis swallowed hard and said, "Yeah, we did," softly. She ran her hands through the coolness of the summer grass.

"I really needed this," she smiled with a youthful grin.

"All I ever wanted was for you to be happy. I always knew you struggled with that," he scooted closer to where she laid. "Willow, I lo...." Before he could finish his statement, she backed away from him and jumped up quickly and ran over to a swing and sat down. She couldn't stand to hear him say those words. She didn't want him to be sweet and kind to her. She didn't deserve that. She swelled with pain inside as she sat in her own pity.

He watched her in her stricken state and grieved in his heart. She had been wounded and wounded badly. Louis knew her story from her childhood very well and understood the things she had been through at a very young age, but there was something else. Something had happened to her that shattered her spirit and the will to fight that he had always admired about her. The damage that was on the inside was extremely visible on the outside. There was no hiding her open wounds. He had forgiven her a long time ago for cheating on him and going to the arms of another man, and the whole time she had pushed him away he refused to let her go. He prayed for her often in hopes that one day she would turn her life back around and return to him.

He had continued to grow in his relationship with the Lord and he and a few of his friends had started a ministry on his campus at school. As he had grown spiritually, he came to the understanding that he had a prophetic gift, and through his prayer and intercession for Willow God had revealed to him some of the calling that was upon her life. The things he saw about her were great, but he was not released to tell her any of it. It wasn't the right time to release that, but he was determined to help as much as he could along the way, not just because God told him to but because his love for her ran deep. "Lord, help me. Please give me the words to say that would heal," he silently prayed. He got up and slowly walked over and grabbed the swing next to Willow.

"You know, God is a miraculous mystery that never ceases to amaze me." He looked across the landscape of the park before he dropped into the swing. "I mean, how can some people look at nature and examine how everything around us naturally work so perfectly together and then say that there's no God?" He chuckled and shook his head as he bent over to play with a clover patch by his shoe. "God is a mastermind, really, pure intelligence and wisdom at its finest. Everything he's made has its own place and purpose. Everything that happens, you better believe there is a reason for it." Willow raised her head and looked in his direction, listening with curiosity.

He looked up at the sky. "You ever think about the birds? They are probably the most envied animal out of the whole animal kingdom because they can fly high in the sky with their beautiful wings. I mean, they can really get up there, and just think about the view of the world that they have when soar above us. They get a perspective of the world that most animals never get a chance to see. Think of its freedom and how it just glides through the wind. Man, what a feeling that must be, huh?" He looked over at Willow, who was staring up at the sky now in wonder. She never took the time to think about that.

He took a deep breath. "With all of the reward and pleasures birds are created to have, it doesn't come without a price. They go through a process of growth that is very painful, which only the strong survive. You see, when the bird has developed enough inside of the egg and it is time for it to come out, it begins to crack the shell with its beak to make an opening. The mother has done all that she can do at this point and the next phase of development for is left up to the baby, no one else. So for the moment her job is done and she has to back away and let her baby make its own entry into the world without any help. The little frail bird must break its way out of the shell all by itself using every muscle that it has and something called an "egg tooth" to break through. It takes some time and it is a major struggle that every bird must go through to get to the next stage of their life. An ignorant person may say that the process is cruel treatment to the baby, and how could the mother be so mean. In actuality the mother knows that breaking the shell is necessary for the motor development of the child. It is the first time that blood is circulated through their wings. If it doesn't go through the pain and struggle of freeing itself, then it will never be strong enough to fly or be independent and so it will inevitably die."

Willow held her head back down but was very intrigued by the story and began to hear the message he was trying to get through to her.

"Willow, I know that you have gone through many hard things in your life and some were not your fault and some were your fault. I don't know if you feel like your life is over or not, but let me reassure you that it's not. You have yet to truly live. What you have gone through has been necessary for your growth and development. It has been the breaking of the shell. The breaking of your own will and the breaking of the old you." She looked up at him and locked her eyes on his. "It is time for the new you to come out. Don't stop fighting through the process. If it has felt like God has left you, He hasn't. He will never leave you. Sometimes He just has to back away and let us go through the breaking of the shell. Trust me... better yet trust God, it is all necessary and it has been for your good. You know, some of the baby birds don't survive through the fight for freedom, because it is a brutal task. And many give up when if they had just given one more push they would have been free. They are blinded by the pain and their current situation that they don't see the progress that they've made and so they just give up and die." He grabbed her face in his hand. "Willow, don't give up baby, you never know when the last push is near to your freedom. You will get through this. Whatever it is. You will get through this. Your wings are being strengthened and when it is the right time you are going to soar like an eagle."

Willow smiled with tears coming down. She lunged into his arms and hugged him tight whispering, "Thank you." She continued, "I need you Louis, I need you with me. I can't do this without you." He pulled away from her after a moment and held his hand behind his back. She leaned back into her swing "What do you have in your hand?" she giggled. He brought his hand forward and opened it. Nestled in the middle of his palm rested a twine of clovers strung together to make a ring. He had stealthily been making it while he was talking. She put her hand over her mouth, remembering how he would always make her a ring out of clovers when he would bring her there. He got down on one knee. "Will you be my wife?"

"You still want me to be your wife?!" she asked in amazement.

"Without a doubt," he quickly answered. He dropped the ring of clovers and reached into his pocket to pull out a small box. Willow jumped up and screamed with excitement. He opened the box and revealed the sparkling diamond ring inside. "I mean it. I want you to be with me forever, putting the past behind us," he said with no hesitation. She grabbed the ring and put it on her finger. She looked at him and then back at her hand. In a flash it had all gotten too real for her. She looked down at him, "Get up for a minute Lou, and sit down. There's some things you should know. I'm not the same girl I was when we were together."

He got up and sat back on the swing, "Look Willow, I am not pressuring you to tell me anything you don't want to. I know who you are."

"Yeah I know, but I want to. I want you to make an informed decision about who you want to spend the rest of your life with. After I tell you this your thoughts of me may change."

"I doubt it, but I do want you to talk about whatever it is that has been eating you up inside so you can get past it."

They sat on the swings until the park closed that evening. She committed to telling him the whole story with Daniel and her pregnancy. Louis sat patiently through the story feeling some of the pain that she had in her heart from what she had been through. He got upset, but after she had finished her confession, they prayed together and he assured her that he wasn't going anywhere.

Over the course of a few months after that they restored their relationship, Willow began to open up and live again. Even though Louis had to go back to school, long distance was no longer a factor because he transferred to a school close to home so that they could be together. Their relationship was tighter than ever. They both flourished together in preparation for their wedding. He encouraged her growth in God and she rededicated her life to Christ. He also wanted her to forgive her mother, and she wanted to as well, but it was still a little hard for her.

THEN, ONCE AGAIN, TRAGEDY struck. One day, Louis was crossing the street to his apartment complex from his car that was parked on the street after a long night of studying for an exam. A drunk driver speeding around the corner didn't see him and hit him head on. The impact was so strong that the hit catapulted him in the air at least four feet away. When he hit the ground, his head bounced off of the pavement, knocking him unconscious. The driver skidded to a stop upon impact and stumbled out of his car and saw Louis on the ground with blood all around. He checked to see if Louis was alive. When he got no response, he looked around and saw that there were no witnesses. Shaken with fear, he ran back into his car and swerved away, never to be found. One of Louis' neighbors finally came out to see what the loud noise was and saw him lying on the ground in a puddle of blood. Running to his rescue, they called for an ambulance.

Around 4:00 that morning Willow was awakened from her sleep by a call from Louis' mother, who briefly explained what had happened, interrupted by her own sobs. Once Willow was told that he was at the hospital in the ICU the phone dropped right out of her hands and she stumbled out of the bed. She didn't bother changing out of her pajamas and she grabbed her coat that was hanging in her closet. She ran down stairs and put on her sneakers that were sitting by the front door. The cool crisp morning air hit her warm face, bringing her rising temperature down. She fumbled with her keys to open her mom's car door, partly because it was hard to see from it still being dark outside, and partly due to her shaking hands. She sped to the hospital on the other side of town as fast as she could, violating every traffic signal.

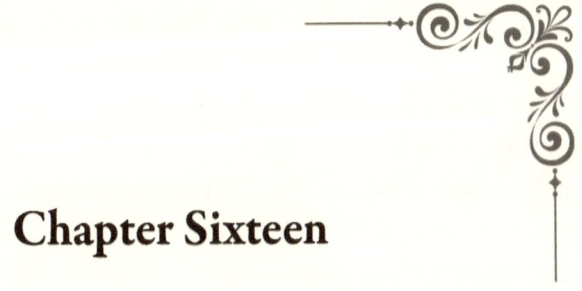

Chapter Sixteen

Once she got there, she found Louis' parents in the ICU floor waiting room. To her surprise, she hadn't cried at all the whole way there, but upon seeing their worried faces Willow fell to her knees in despair. It took Louis' mother and father both along with some nurses to calm her down. After she was completely settled his mother sat her down and told her about his condition.

"The doctor said that he has broken both of his legs, his ribs, and he has a fractured skull with a concussion," Mrs. Brown said while rubbing Willow's back.

"Oh my goodness. Is he...?" Willow said in shock.

"Wait, Willow, there's more. His left hip and shoulder come out of socket as well, because that was the side in which he had been hit on. But the doctors performed surgery on him early this morning right when he got rushed into the hospital. That's a blessing! And the doctors said that he was looking very strong." Mrs. Brown said softly. She tried to give herself and Willow some hope, but she was doing a poor job. Nothing she could say would settle Willow.

"Well, good, he's ok! Can I go see him?" Willow jumped out of her chair.

Mrs. Brown gave her husband a heart wrenching look and then lowered her head, not giving any eye contact to Willow. "You can go see him, but he's in a coma and the doctors don't know when or if he will come out."

The days turned to weeks and the weeks turned to months. It had been four months since Louis' accident and he was still trapped in the coma. For the first two months of his condition Willow was committed to going and sitting with him all day long and spending many nights alongside him at the hospital. She would pray and read to him constantly. After a while hopelessness, who she knew all too well, came back, and this time he was there to stay. She saw no improvement in Louis and the doctors began to talk to his parents about pulling the plug, but they refused to even think about it. It was way too much for her to handle and she became angry once again at God. She fell back in to her dark world and confined herself in her room to never be seen by the world again.

"LISTEN TO ME!" HE WALKED over to Willow and put his hands on her shoulders then looked straight into her eyes. His touch awakened her from her daydream, bringing her back to reality. "You have a great opportunity right now. You can right all of your wrongs, but only if you eat from the fruit from this tree. You have the opportunity to go back and live a great and prosperous life. You can have riches and fame, you can come back and have everything you have ever wanted. And we can be together, just you and I. Oh, Willow, can't you see! God wants you to have your heart's desire. You could be as wise as Solomon, knowing all things, just think of the possibilities." He took her hand in his and turned to lead her the last few steps towards the tree. They stopped right up under the shade of some of its thick branches. One of the branches drooped down due to the weight of the big ripe peach that hung from it. Louis reached up and yanked the peach to free it. Willow's stomach growled as she drooled over the plumpness of the fruit.

"We can go back together," he said as he held out the peach in his hand for her to take. She stepped towards him while the smell of the sweet peach drew her closer. She grabbed the fruit from his hand, which made his eyes dilated in extreme excitement. She pulled the peach up to her mouth and its fuzzy skin brushed against her lips.

"WONDER HOW SHE'S DOING," Petundan said, looking down at Willow's limp body.

"All we can do is hope for the best and be ready for whatever comes. We have been commanded to protect her on this side, and that my friend is what we are going to do at all cost," Michael said, shifting from left to right in his battle stance, squeezing his sword. He was ready for action as he closely watched Death, who stared back at him in silent rage. Death led the demons in a slow haunting march, circling the bubble that divided the two enemies. The ground began to shake, causing the house to shake with a rhythmic vibration. The demons laughed and taunted their opponents. Shrieking wildly and jumping up and down, they all scattered, making room for the floor to part as a black hole formed in the ground. The two angels that guarded Willow watched, dreading what was to come.

Suddenly, dark beings with wings and black stringy tentacles around their bodies rose up from the mouth of the gaping hole in the floor. Their oblong heads were drastically bigger than their slim bodies, making them look like flying extra-terrestrial beings. "Fallen angels," Michael said as he lowered his head. Five fallen angels came through the portal and then it quickly closed up. They flew, swarming round and around the bubble, like vultures awaiting their prey. Their big hollow eyes stared down at Petundan and the archangel Michael.

As the dark beings continued to marched and fly around the room, they chanted praises to Lucifer. They raised their voices louder and louder with each step. Michael could feel the evil crawling in, but he was prepared. The blood shield that created the hedge of protection around the two angels and Willow began to become thinner and thinner by the second.

"What's happening?" Petundan yelled.

"I don't know, something's wrong. Willow may be on the wrong path, but I haven't gotten any new instruction. So we still have to make sure nothing happens to her," Michael answered.

The blood finally disappeared out of sight and the demonic force's chanting and movement came to an abrupt halt. The two angels looked at each other in shock.

Michael remained cool and gave Petundan a silent message as he shuffled his eyes to the left. Petundan understood, taking a brief pause, then he began to spin around rapidly as his wings of steel were still open as far as they could go, moving to the left of the room. Sharp stakes of steel emerged out of his wings making his shield a lethal weapon. As he spun around, demons were knocked over and some were stabbed by the metal spikes that protruded from his armor.

At the same moment Michael struck to the right and severed the head of an approaching demon clean off with one stroke of his blade. As its body bent over to fall, Michael leaped up and bounced on it with one foot, which catapulted him high in the air. This gave him leverage to thrust his sword into the belly of a fallen one that hovered over them. He sliced the creature in two by slashing his weapon from its belly button straight up to its forehead. The insides of the creature splattered across the room. The remaining four shrieked and frantically flapped their wings in anguish from the demise of their ally. They all charged towards him at once, moving left and right to dodge the horrid spin attack of Petundan's wings. Petundan increased his speed, causing a strong wind to form, throwing the demonic flying army off balance.

Death jumped up from the chaos and knocked the fallen angels down out of the air with the hammer figure that protruded from his head. He looked down at them. "This one is mine!" He flared his nose and stared intensely at Michael. Michael stared back with the same fierce energy, twirling his sword around in his hand. Death bent over and began to charge straight at him head first. He hit Michael in the stomach with his hammer head and grabbed his legs and slammed him into the wall. The wall cracked from the impact and Michael grunted in pain. Petundan finally stopped spinning and looked to see Michael's status. Petundan saw that he wasn't doing too good and grew weary. "What is going on my Lord?! What happened to our protection?" he shouted up to the heavens. Just as he was distracted, one of the demons that was still standing slashed Petundan's face with his claw.

"WOE TO THOSE WHO ARE wise in their own eyes and clever in their own sight! Woe to those who call evil good and good evil; that put darkness for light and light for darkness; that put bitter for sweet and sweet for bitter! DO NOT be deceived by the thief. For he comes to steal, kill, and destroy you." The voice no longer a whisper but a shout in the wind. She stopped and pulled the fruit away from her mouth. "Hey! What are you doing?" he said with disappointment. "Stop playing Willow, this is it your last chance. Which will it be, Hell or freedom, famine or fame?" he asked with anxiety.

The voice in the wind came back. "No man can serve two masters, ye cannot serve God and mammon." She shook on the inside from the voices' last statement because it was scripture she knew all too well.

Turning around towards the gaping walkway to the home of the deserted land and lonely tree, there was the most beautiful blinding light shining through. Willow felt it was calling her to come and see the treasures it held. She turned back to Louis and saw that his eyes were switching back and forth from light green to indigo, like a glitch in the matrix. "You're not Louis," she said, backing away and shaking her head. "I don't want any part of this. You eat the fruit yourself! I don't want to be God. Jesus is more than enough for me." She dropped the peach and it fell to the ground, splatting open revealing its rotted flesh.

DEATH PICKED MICHAEL up off the ground and lifted him over his head. Suddenly complete darkness took over the room and the earth shook. All of the fighting and scuffling came to a stop. A thunderous voice spoke with wrath, "Let there be light!" Ultra-white light blasted through the room from corner to corner. When Michael and Petundan's eyes adjusted, they saw that each of the evil presences in the room were statues, paralyzed in place. Their flesh had turned to stone, sizzling in the light.

Michael was still dangling in the air, bound in the hands of Death. "Uhhh... I need a little help, Lord!"

"Go back to where you belong!" the voice rumbled through the air. The statues crumbled into piles of ash from the sheer vibration of Yahweh's voice. Michael dropped to the floor with a thud. He got up and dusted himself off. "You're always right on time. Thank you, Yahweh." The piles of ash turned into leeches crawling on the floor. A powerful suction of force pulled them into a portal opening in the floor. The gaping mouth of the portal swallowed every last one up and then concealed itself as if nothing had occurred. Right after, there was a knock at the door.

WILLOW TURNED AROUND to run back towards the light and heard a loud screech from behind her. She looked back as she ran and saw that the imposter had begun to shift its appearance once more. Now it was unable to conceal how it really looked or the surge of rage it carried. His body became a dark green that was a cross between scales and rubber in texture. He had a long lanky tail and boney ripples sticking out on his back. There were only small holes where his nose was supposed to be and his eyes glowed yellow like a cat with green veins running through them. His pupils were slant black ovals. He was a reptile of some sort who stood on two feet, hissing like a snake with a long slithering tongue.

Willow picked up her speed, eager to get away from the hideous sight as the serpent glided through the tall grass after her with ease. As she ran, the beautiful scenery shifted and changed like a jigsaw puzzle being dismantled.

A single snowflake fell from the now overcast sky and landed on Willow's shoulder. She cried out in pain, for the flake burned at the touch. She looked over at her shoulder and the snow had eaten clean through the cloth of her shirt and steam flowed up from the burn she now wore. More began to fall and everything around her became covered in a blanket of the burning snow in a matter of seconds. The land that once spoke of abundance now only told the story of lack.

Willow's run turned into a hop because the snow on the ground scorched through her shoes to her feet. Then a strong gusty wind swirled around her, lifting her off the ground and pulling her closer to the light. "NO!! She's mine! She belongs to me!" Lucifer hissed with anxiety. He screamed, "She's mine" over and over, and each time his voice got deeper and deeper.

The wind safely placed her at the entrance of the seemingly bare field of mustard seeds. Willow looked back and saw by that time dark figures with wings had come out of the forest and had joined Lucifer in the middle of the meadow behind her. He shouted a command in his foreign language, pointing towards her, and the fallen angels charged in formation.

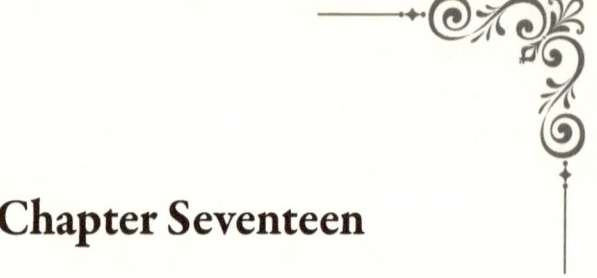

Chapter Seventeen

S he turned back around to walk through the entryway when she was stopped by two tall beings guarding the door. Before her were two ten foot angels standing on either side of the opening. They stood at attention like soldiers awaiting their next command. In their hands each held a sword that carried a swirling ring of fire extending from the tip all the way down to the handle. They held their sword clasped together, forming an x to block the way into the mysterious land.

Now that she was up close, Willow understood where the sparkling light was coming from. It was their wings, that were made of golden feathers rustling in the breeze that blew by. The one on the right side came out of position and bent down towards Willow. The angel looked her up and down and then gazed deep into her eyes. The angel flinched back and said, "You do not belong here. You may not enter."

She looked over her shoulder and saw the darkness drawing closer. She spotted the once beautiful magnificent tree that bore the gigantic fruit and gasped with disbelief. The tree was still big, but it was black, and now in exchange for the juicy fruit, human heads of lost souls hung upon its branches. She could hear their anguishing screams in the distance.

In desperation she cried out with her eyes closed in prayer, "Have mercy on me Oh Lord; I do believe. Show me your way!" The two angels that stood protecting the entrance lifted their swords of fire up high in the air, clearing the way for Willow to enter.

THE BEDROOM DOOR SLOWLY opened, "Willow are you up?" Stephen had been praying for his granddaughter all morning and felt the need to drop by and talk with her. He stepped into the room and saw Willow laid out on the floor. "Willow!" he shouted as he ran to her side. Michael and Petundan rejoiced, singing praises to God as they watched. For they knew Willow had made her choice and she had done well.

WILLOW QUICKLY RAN into the opening of the field to safety. Lucifer and his company ran up to the pathway, only to be blocked by the two angels and their swords of flames. He stood and watched her intensely through the gaps between the angels' swords with his allegiance behind him. "This is not over," he hissed bubbling fury.

Willow stopped and looked behind her, making sure that she was protected from the evil that had chased her moments before. With her attackers no longer in sight, she turned ahead and focused on the bare tree that stood lonely in the middle of the open field. She examined the area and looked down to see that the ground had no grass to blow in the wind and no flowers waiting to bloom. It was just a dry, dirty plane with a blanket of small seeds that scattered off into the distance.

As she walked towards the tree, a heaviness she had never felt before came over her. It was not only a physical weight that caused her to lean from side to side as she fought to regain control of her own body, but the heaviness reached into the inner depths of her heart, causing her to wail in a deep sob. Her sobs grew louder with each aching moan as the weight drew her closer to the ground, making her stumble as she continued to walk forward. Knowing sorrow very well, none of it had ever compared to this. She didn't understand what was causing all of the pain she felt. It was indescribable, like she was being crushed but yet embraced at the same time. Despite the growing weakness of her legs, she pressed on towards the frail tree, which was only a blurry figure to her now because of the multitude of tears clouding her vision.

After a while she could no longer lift her head. All she could focus on was her shoes treading over and kicking the small bead like seeds along the ground. When she finally approached her destination, the presence bore down on her with greater force. Her knees gave out and she hit the ground, causing dirt and debris to fly up in a gust of wind around her. Crawling up closer, she noticed a red puddle of liquid around the base of the trunk. Her face was so close to ground by then she was able to quickly solve the mystery of the unknown substance. It was blood, but to her surprise, it didn't startle her. She glided her hand over the liquid, then another drop of blood fell into the puddle from above, causing a splash. Then more came down causing, small splashes in the puddle wherever they fell.

Willow used all of the strength she could muster and lifted herself up onto her knees. For a moment with her head lowered she took in a deep breath. Then, she raised her head to see what was coming from the sky. Many drops of blood rained down sporadically. Some even fell on her face as she continued to cry uncontrollably, with eyes fixed on the mangled body twisted and hanging on the tree. The wounds that covered the body made it impossible to make any observation of His physical features, beaten beyond recognition and naked with nothing to cover up but a ripped piece of cloth. The body was literally torn to pieces as small fragments of ripped flesh fell down and splashed in the pool of blood on the ground. His arms were stretched out wide along the length of the only two branches that the tree owned, pointing out east and west as if they were the rope in a malicious game of tug o' war.

As her eyes beheld the horrific sight, a revelation came to her and she began to understand why her walk there was so labored. She was in the presence of the Lord, in His glory. She wasn't worthy to even lay eyes upon Him, even in the tormented state He appeared to be in at the moment. Willow understood that it was pure mercy and a privilege that she was granted to behold him in this state. And she did not take it for granted. She saw how much of a fool she was, because she was selfish enough to take her own life when the precious life before her had been given freely so that she could live. She felt how small and undeserving she was, realizing how badly she had broken His heart by rejecting the love that she had always desired. His eyes locked with hers in a hypnotic gaze.

Willow noticed that even though His body was beaten badly and He struggled weakly to inhale each hollow breath, His eyes were full of life and bright as the rays of the sun. She couldn't look away, not even for a second. Through the fixated gaze upon her, He told the story of love without uttering a single word. He showed her how He was lied to and conspired against, even by some who had walked closely with Him. She saw how He had been beaten and called names. How He was mocked and taunted with no relent. In His eyes she saw her reflection and understood that He shielded her from that penalty. All the things He endured should have been for her, but He stood in her place.

With sadness Willow screamed, "No more please! I can't take it." She squeezed her eyes tightly shut and shook her head rapidly. Then she heard a voice say, "This light affliction is but for a moment, it is all for a greater glory. Don't fret, my child, this was written and so it was fulfilled. It was for you, my daughter." The words cover over her like a blanket and she was comforted. She hadn't felt so safe since her father was alive. She opened her eyes and her faith was revived.

Tears dropped from His eyes as he slowly melted into the trunk of the tree until His image disappeared. A single bolt of lightning struck the ground inches away from where she sat. She screamed and shifted back, frightened by the spontaneous event. The ground rumbled and shook like an earthquake, drinking up the puddle of blood around the trunk of the tree with a loud slurping sound. By this time Willow was on her feet, staring at the ground, waiting on high alert.

After all of the blood was gone the once frail tree grew high above the clouds. The trunk expanded thick and stable and stretched higher and higher as a multitude of branches reached out in every direction. Dark green leaves grew and nine pieces of fruit began to form amongst the branches. The fruit grew so big they dropped to the ground, breaking the branches in which they hung. One of them rolled up to her foot and she saw that something was written on it. She picked it up and read "love" aloud, which was engraved in its flesh. Looking at the rest of the fruit on the ground, she discovered that they all wore their own inscription. Willow read them all, wondering what it all meant. "Long-suffering, Patience, Joy, Peace, Goodness, Faithfulness, Self-control, and Gentleness."

Looking at the fruit of love that she held in her hand and realizing how famished she was, she decided to take a bite. She didn't think she had anything to lose and it looked good enough to fill her empty stomach. As she was about to take a bite a voice called out to her, "Willow." The Earth shook once more, causing the tall tree to stretch out even more into different abstract shapes and colors. Willow could see that the tree was turning into something totally new. When the transformation was complete an image of a man made of water stood before her. She was extremely still, afraid of showing any sign of life. Only her hand that held the fruit shook, causing it to fall to the ground, rolling away from her.

"Hello, Willow." The mysterious man gave her a joyous smile and walked toward her. Willow found comfort in the strange being, sensing He was friendly. Recognizing His voice of the wind that had previously helped her escape the deception of evil, she forgot to be afraid.

"Who...What are you?" she hesitantly asked.

The man chuckled in amusement as he approached her. She resisted the urge to poke her finger into His arm, but she was curious if she would get wet from a single touch. The water glided and splashed with each move He took. *How is this possible? A man made of water,* she thought.

"Sometimes I am water, sometimes I drift in the wind, sometimes I can even present myself as fire. It just depends on what is needed at the time," he responded to her pondering thoughts. "Just know that I am one of the same of He that is in the beginning of creation and that shall always be. I am the sent one, the helper."

"Huh?" Willow scratched her head and the peculiar being laughed.

"It's okay, Willow," he reassured.

Willow marveled at His carefree bubbly nature and how He acted so familiar with her, as if He had always known her. He embodied a light attitude; she would have given anything to know what that felt like.

"You talk to me as if you already know me."

"Of course, I know you. I have always been with you, interceding for you and helping you along the way."

Annoyed by His statement, Willow asked, "If you were really helping me as you say, then how come I struggled so much? I never saw you."

"Just because I am with you doesn't mean that you will be free from pain and tribulations. No matter how hard things get, there is always someone going through something much harder than you, remember that. Anyway, I communicated with the Father on your behalf numerous times when you were not even thinking about Him. He loves you so much that he intervened in spite of your inability to acknowledge Him. I would have helped more, but only those who open their hearts to me will hear when I speak. Only those who accept and welcome me in will be sensitive to the pull when I lead them in the right direction. It all comes down to you and your ignorance or refusal to let me in. I can't make the decision for you." A compassionate smile came over His face. "I wanted to help you so much more. I was grieved time and time again because you wouldn't just ask for my help. You stopped believing."

"I did and I'm so very sorry that I hurt you, but I didn't know you then and I barely know you now. Who did you say you were again?" Willow questioned in her own lack of knowledge.

"Listen, I know that you're not that familiar with me yet. In time you will get to know me very well. You and I have much work to do, but I will go into that at another time. I have many names with many abilities. For now, you will know me as Holy Spirit, the gift who bears many gifts for all who desire."

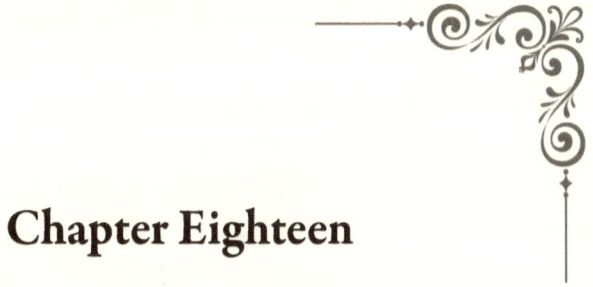

Chapter Eighteen

"Oh yeah, I know who you are. It makes sense now. This fruit on the ground, it all belongs to you, right?"

"Correct!" he said excitedly. "They are all representations of traits that are added to all vessels who let me in. This fruit and my special gifts are all evidence that I am with you. I know that you have heard a little about who I am, but now it is time for you to experience who I am. But first..."

Holy Spirit held out his hand. "I am so happy that you were able to hear me back there and you took heed. No matter how much the evil serpent threw your way. All of heaven rejoices this day because you do have ears to hear the word of the Lord. But not just to hear, but most importantly, to carry out the word of the Lord. And now, there is someone who is waiting to talk with you."

Willow took His hand and noticed that her hand was consumed by the water. A sweet cooling came over her. She took in a deep breath and embraced the feeling.

"Why here? Why would the Lord be in such a dry and dreary place?" Willow asked as they walked through the field.

"Ha! Good question! Let this be your first lesson from me. Things are not always as they seem, not here and especially not back in the natural realm. Just because something may present itself as beauty doesn't mean beauty is what it is made of. And on the flip side, just because something may look lacking and unappealing does not mean that it doesn't have an abundance of valuable riches. The lust of your eyes deceives man too many times. Do not be tempted by appearances and things that are temporary in value. You have to dig beyond the surface to experience the true essence of person, place or thing.

All the things that Lucifer tried to get you to partake of, such as fame and fortune, will all pass away one day. But the things that I will give you are eternal and most of them you can not see, taste, hear, smell or touch. I say to you; the weak things are chosen to confound the things which are mighty. Sometimes you must look for Me in the most unlikely places and there you will find Me." Holy Spirit spoke, still holding Willows hand as they casually strolled along the field.

"That is so backwards. It doesn't make sense. The way something looks should correlate with the truth of what it is. But I guess that's what it means when people say "don't judge a book by the cover" or better yet, when my grandpa would always say, "When a situation looks like it is getting worse most times things are actually getting better." It still doesn't make since though; it seems like God wants us to be tricked." Willow said in frustration.

"That couldn't be further from the truth! Our Father which is in heaven wants you to seek Him, for His ways are not your ways. He doesn't want you to fail. He wants you to be set apart from the world and to be transformed by the renewing of your mind. The carnal mind is what tells you that everything that looks good is good, and this is simply a lie. The world has twisted you and has turned you from My righteous way of thinking. The world is foolish in calling those things that are right wrong and what is wrong right. Come with Me, beloved, and I will teach you the path of righteousness; let the veil be lifted off of your eyes."

They continued to walk a few steps, then Holy Spirit stopped. He sensed something was out of place. He looked straight into Willow's eyes. "Willow, your heart is black and torn and it's of stone. You can't go on this way. You won't receive all that We have to show and give you. Your unwillingness to forgive has corrupted your heart, causing hate to have its way. The misfortune that you have experienced has consumed you." His voice was a mixture of concern and conviction. Willow thought about the disfigured image she had seen in the window of truth. Then she thought over the span of her life and all the people that had hurt her. Her mom, Daniel, and Nicole... up until that point she had not noticed that she was still angry at them.

"How do you forgive? Thinking about it now, I realize that I don't know how, especially when the person who has hurt me doesn't even acknowledge it or refuses to apologize. They go on with their life as if nothing happened," she said with a shaky voice. Then a dark shadow came over her and she was enraged. "NO! I won't forgive them. Why should I? I never did anything to them! I mean, take Daniel for instance, all I did was love him and look what he did to me!!" As she continued, she lost control and her countenance turned dark and sinister. "NOOO!" she screamed with rage "I won't do it. I hate...." Holy Spirit gently placed His hand over her heart and she became quite mid-sentence. The dark shadow vanished off of her and she came back to herself.

"Whoa, what was that?" she asked still gaining her composure.

"I examined your heart and brought to the surface what was hidden deep inside. I allowed you to see a glimpse of the wickedness you carry within." He removed his hand from her chest, leaving behind a wet hand print on her shirt.

"I don't want that inside of me! That's not who I am! Help me to understand. How do I forgive?" Willow begged.

"You must let go Willow. Let Me take over. You cannot do it within your own strength, for the heart is deceitfully wicked. Allow Me to soften your heart so that it may be transformed and made flesh once more. Your unwillingness to forgive opens the door for hatred and a legion of other evil spirits to have their way within you," Holy Spirit explained.

"I am reminded of a parable that Jesus told his disciples, about the king who wanted to settle accounts with his servants. As he...."

"Oh yeah, I know that parable about forgiveness, my grandpa's pastor used to always go over it in his sermons. I think it is in the book of Mathew," Willow interrupted excitedly. "Let see, it's about how the King was getting a settlement for a debt from someone who owed him, but the man didn't have the money he owed. He begged the king to let him pay him later and the King showed him mercy and canceled his debt. But then that same man went to settle a debt that someone else owed him. The debtor didn't have the money that he owed him and begged to be able to pay at a later time. The man refused and showed him no mercy. Matter of fact I think he threw him in jail. When the King got word of what happened he called for the man and asked why he didn't show mercy for his fellow servant as he had showed mercy upon him. In anger the King threw the man in jail to be tortured until he could pay back his debt to him."

"That is right, Willow! This is how the Heavenly Father is. He is faithful and merciful to forgive you of every sin that you commit, but if you do not forgive those who have wronged you or those you feel owe you, He will surely not forgive you. You may not like what I am about to say, but I assure you it is the truth." He walked forward a few steps and turned around to face her. "Willow, you are not perfect; you have done wrong also, just like those who have hurt you. And sometimes you have done worse. What about all of them?" He took a long pause. "The ones who laid awake crying a night because of something you did or said. I assure you, you have broken some hearts and have caused some pain in others' lives as well. What about them? Have you gone and apologized to the ones that you know of?"

Willow didn't answer, but looked down in shame.

"I didn't think so. Then why do you feel it's necessary to get an apology in order to forgive someone, when you yourself have not extended that same apology to all YOU have hurt? It is time to face yourself and accept responsibility for what has happened instead of blaming everyone else. Then you can forgive the person you are really holding a grudge for... yourself."

Willow couldn't believe it. That was it. She had been holding hatred in her heart all this time for herself. That's why she couldn't move on; she was sabotaging herself and stifling her progress in life this whole time. Maybe that was why it had been so easy for her to take the pills that morning. She began to understand what Holy Spirit was telling her and the truth cut her immensely.

Holy Spirit continued, "Forgiveness is not contingent on the action of others and it is not a pass that says what the other person did was ok. But it is given freely out of unconditional love, the love of God. It comes from a place inside of you that never runs dry, but is overflowing in abundance. Now, I have heard people say that forgiveness is not for the other person but for yourself. Please do not get caught up in this lie. If that statement were true, that would mean that forgiveness is wrapped in selfishness and not in love, and this is simply not true. When the Lord forgives you, do you think it's for Him or for your benefit? All of God's creation is connected and your journey in life affects many others' journeys. When you hold un-forgiveness towards someone you not only stifle your spiritual growth and blessing, but you cause a negative effect on the other person's spiritual growth. It may not seem like it because you could see that person that did something to you a year later and it seems like they are on top of the world. But remember the first lesson, everything is not always what it seems to be."

Willow soaked up every word that Holy Spirit spoke to her, and his words fed her soul. She felt so light she thought she would drift off into the distance by the smallest gust of wind. "True forgiveness is an act of agape love that is freely given as the father freely pours out his mercy new each and every day."

She looked up at Him, "I never thought about it that way. Thank you. It's a tough pill to swallow, but I think I get it."

Holy Spirit smiled, "I knew you would. You learn very quickly; that's how I know you will do well! When I touched you, I imparted some of myself to you. Your heart is softening and becoming whole again." Willow knew that what he said was true, because she could feel the difference radiating inside of her.

They started to walk again until a big grassy hill came into view. "Now it is time for you to move on in your journey. I have enjoyed our time together and I am sure we will get more time later." Holy Spirit pointed at a man who stood on top of the grassy hill above where they stood. "Your Shepherd awaits you. He will lead you the rest of the way."

When Willow approached the hill, she looked up and saw Jesus standing at the top, dressed in a tan mantle made of sheep skin. He held a long wooden staff in His right hand and a long rod with a knob on the end in the other. His back was facing her as He watched the sunset in the horizon. The soft oranges and pinks in the sky glowed upon His sun kissed skin. His long, loosely curled hair gently tussled in the passing breeze. She started to walk up the hill and He turned around, looking back at her with a welcoming smile. There was no trace of the mangled man before who was thrown on the tree. He was strong and stood tall with a faint glow of virtue on his face. His hazel eyes were the only thing that remained from the horrible sight in the field earlier. She was sure because she would never forget the fire of love that flowed through them.

Excitement came over Him as he saw her coming up the hill towards Him. He ran towards her with his arms extended widely. "Willow!" He shouted with joy. Comfort rose up within her and she quickened her pace towards Him. She felt like there was an invisible gravitational pull between them that got stronger as she jogged toward him. They quickly reached each other and Jesus wrapped His arms around her, dropping the staff and rod in His hands. He picked her up, swinging her around in a tight embrace. Willow felt deeply undeserving of His embrace, but she enjoyed the endearing gesture and wished it would last forever.

He finally put her down and said, "I have waited for the day when we would meet like this. I am so happy that you chose to come here!" He took her in His arms again. He hugged her so tightly that Willow began to struggle for air. He let her go and held her out at arm's length, looking at her like a proud father. Then He took her back in his arms for one more embrace. They both giggled.

"I am so glad that you are happy to see me. I thought you would be upset with me," Willow said as she rested her head on His chest. "There is nothing you can ever do that will separate you from Me." He let her go. "The first thing you should know is that I am the complete opposite of your assumptions. So throw out all you think you know, because I am so very proud of you." Jesus took her by the hand. "Come, we will talk as we walk. Come, I will lead you to your appointment. You don't want to be late."

"Appointment? Who am I supposed to meet?" Willow questioned, still a little worried.

"Don't be worried, Beloved. The Lord is with you. My word will be a lamp unto your feet and a light unto your path."

They walked and talked as people who had known each other for years, as close friends. "You know, Willow, I am one hundred percent God, but I am also one hundred percent man. I understand every single thing that you have ever felt. I know what it is to endure the struggles of life. You can talk to me about anything."

"Yeah, I know what you're going to say... God never puts more on you than you can bear, right?" Willow said condescendingly.

Jesus looked at her and tilted His head in a questioning fashion. He stared at her face searching for some type of explanation of what she had just said. Willow cleared her throat and could feel her face warming up with embarrassment. She knew she had said something wrong, but didn't know exactly what.

"Umm, you know, God never puts more on you than you can bear?" she now questioned. "At least that is what my grandfather would always tell me, and I would hear a lot of other believers say it too."

Jesus shook His head, "What you have just said is not in the scriptures and is not truth. It is a twisting of the word of God. But it *is* written that, "God is faithful, who will not suffer you to be tempted above that ye are able to bear; but will with the temptation also make a way to escape, that ye may be able to bear it." This scripture pertains to temptation and How the Lord will not let you be tempted more than you are able to bear. The truth of the matter is that in life you will go through many hardships, some great and some small. Many are way too hard to handle on your own. And guess what? That is the very point of it all. The Father wants you to depend on Him to get through them. When I walked the Earth, I was constantly praying to Father. I had to seek Him to get through the hardships of life on Earth. He wants to be acknowledged in your weakness, actually in all things, for He is the Strong Tower. So it is written: Lean not unto your own understanding but in all your ways acknowledge the Lord and He will direct your path. You know, it hurts my heart when the twisting of the word takes place, because a simple misleading of the truth can turn someone away from me. Those who are deceived will think that I am a liar when horrific tragedy happens in their life. They run away saying "Where is God? I thought he wouldn't put more on you than you can bear, so there must not be a God," when all they have to do is run to me and I will give them rest. So yes, Willow, sometimes you will go through more than you can bear, but if you acknowledge Me those hard times will only humble you and bring you closer to Me."

"Wow, that makes much more sense to me," Willow said, shaking her head up and down. "Man...I thought my grandfather had all of the right answers when it came to You."

"Yes, even the strongest in the faith can get some things wrong. That is why it's important to study and show yourself approved. Too many times the church grabs ahold of what someone is saying in the world and runs with it because they think that's gonna bring more people into their church. They don't even check to see if it lines up with the prophecies or with what I've said. To tell you the truth Willow, I am not impressed."

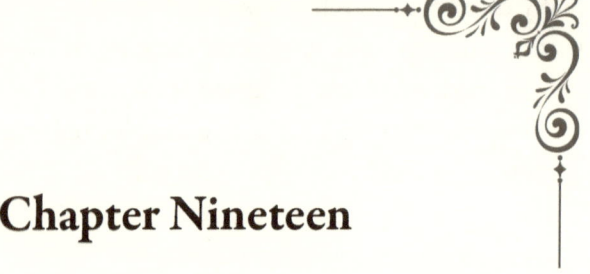

Chapter Nineteen

The two continued to walk and talk. Willow was so captivated by the teachings of Jesus that she didn't notice when they approached the property of a small house. Jesus stopped and slowly motioned towards the house, "This is your resting place for the evening." She looked across the way at the dark old shack. She could barely make out any details of the house because there was a thick mist seeping from the inside through the cracks of the front door and windows, surrounding its perimeter.

"I'm supposed to sleep in there? By myself? Wait, but I thought I had an appointment!" she demanded, looking back at Jesus.

"Oh ye of little faith, have you not learned to trust me yet? You are never alone, and don't worry you will not miss your appointment. It will begin once you step inside, but before you go you must take off your shoes for this is holy ground," Jesus instructed.

Willow did as she was told and took off her shoes. She began to walk towards the house but then looked back at Jesus. She ran back to Him, "I just wanted to say something before I go. I am so sorry for how I took my life for granted. I was so selfish this whole time and I didn't stand for what was right. And then I tried to take my own life abandoning all that You stand for. Now I see how much of a fool I was. Please forgive me for not taking you seriously. It is such a honor to have life and I gave up so easily." With tears in her eyes she continued, "I didn't even allow my child a chance to live." Jesus smiled at her and took her in his arms. "I have already forgiven you before you even asked and you know what, the child that you speak of is with me and is well. And know this, above all my desire for you is that your mind is changed, renewed. No longer compromising, living as the world does. That you turn away from those old ways and never want them anymore. Becoming a new person, transformed into a new creature that is dependent on Me. This is true repentance. Now go, your slate is wiped clean. You are made free."

Willow turned and walked steadily up the pathway leading to the porch of the house with a new joy that she had never experienced before. Once she stood on the porch the mist overtook her and she lost all stability in her legs. There was a weight in the thickness of the atmosphere that was greater than what she had experienced before at the tree in the field. Crawling on her hands and knees, she felt like hours had passed by the time she made it to the front door.

Once she crawled inside of the house, she managed to brace herself to stand. Up on both feet, she got a better view of her resting place. There was only one big main room with no furniture and no pictures on the walls. Willow thought it creepy that the place was completely bare. Angled in the left corner of the house was a burning bush that did not get consumed by the fire it yielded. She was still and nervous with fear, not knowing how to react. The phenomenon made her remember the story of Moses and how God showed himself to him through the burning bush. "So it is true," she whispered. Willow had always thought it was absurd that a burning bush could talk. So, she had never believed the story, but she was being made a believer of many things today.

"I have covered more of Myself so I do not harm your flesh," a deep distinguished voice spoke out and filled the room. The flames flickered and grew higher with each inflection. She fell to her knees with her head bowed. "I AM that I AM, the Alpha and Omega and I have chosen you." The house shook as He spoke. Willow's heartbeat became harder and faster as he spoke.

"You have turned from me time and time again, but still I have chosen you. You have tried to end your life, but I AM the one who giveth and taketh away. I decide who lives and who dies. You have tried to run away from believing in me, but I AM the author and finisher of your faith. I AM the Sovereign God. I AM in control and nothing happens that I do not know about!"

Without thinking Willow lifted her head and immediately responded, "Well, then why did you let my father get sick with that thing attached to him and let him die?" Willow slapped both of her hands over her mouth in shock. She couldn't believe she had just challenged God in such a disrespectful way. She squeezed her eyes shut and fell on her face expecting His wrath to be unleashed.

An unsettling came over the room and the quietness spoke louder than God's own voice. She expected fire, brimstone, ANYTHING other than complete silence. The only thing heard was the crackling of the fire in the bush.

"Rise up to your feet, daughter," He finally said. Willow slowly stood up, surprised by the calmness of the Lord's approach. "I know that you are angry with Me. You place the blame on Me for what happened to your father and for many things that have happened in your life. Willow, I love David deeply. He died because it was time for him to pass on. You must trust me when I tell you that it is all according to the plan. There is a bigger picture that you cannot see right now. Your view of the puzzle is limited by YOUR circumstances and by the things that only concern YOU. I see the whole condition and I know the expected end. You see me as a God who takes pleasure in destruction and chaos in the world because you think that I am doing nothing about it. As if I am some big tyrant laughing at the demise of my people. Things are not always what they seem."

Willow interrupted, "Yeah, I know. Holy Spirit drilled that one in pretty good."

"I hurt when my people hurt. In a perfect world, the way I originally intended, the things that happened to your father would have never happened. The evil stronghold on your father would have never had access to him. But there were great ramifications in the spirit and natural that took place during the fall of man through Adam. Unfortunately, it has hindered your quality of life. The sinful nature became a part of you, deceiving you into thinking that you, yourselves, are God. You see, the whole purpose of me giving you free will was for us to be in true relationship with one another. I always knew there was a possibility that you could go your own way, but I gave you free will anyway."

"Why did you risk giving us free will if you knew that there was a chance that we would turn away from you?" Willow had never really understood that concept.

"Well, let me ask you this, if you had the ability to control the actions of others would you *MAKE* someone love you and be around you, or would you rather them love you for who you are and because they chose to do so from their own heart and mind?"

Willow thought for a minute; *what an odd question.* She never before took the time to think about how God felt and the price He paid for loving us so much and wanting to be loved by us.

"I would want them to choose to love me on their own without any of my control," Willow whispered.

"Yes, exactly!" the Lord said excitedly. "That is the whole intent; I wanted true worship, true relationship, true love with my children, not robots! And that, to me, was worth the risk. And yes, Adam and Eve were deceived and went against me, but I was not shaken or caught off guard by it. I already knew the cost and the measures I was willing to take to restore my relationship with man before they ever took the forbidden bite. It was my pleasure to give my only son, the unblemished lamb, the ultimate sacrifice to reconnect us back together. See Willow, love is all about the humility of sacrifice. I willingly sacrificed some of my control and gave you free will. I graciously sacrificed my only son, who is the most precious part of myself wrapped in flesh, to the world. Jesus also willingly sacrificed his life on the cross for the sins of all who believe. The process of life is not about what happens to you, but about your response to the hard situations that arise against you. It's to see if you are able to willing sacrifice your will for Mine. Life on Earth is only for a mere moment, but it does not end there. It is just a testing of my children's capacity to come back to me in a wicked world that tries to keep us separated."

"Well Lord, I AM that I AM," Willow cleared her throat, being extra formal and correct in her approach to her creator. "People have told me before that we shouldn't question You, God, but I was wondering, why did you forbid Adam and Eve from eating from the tree of the knowledge of Good and Evil? You didn't want us to know good from evil?"

"Hmm, that answer goes beyond your ability to understand, but I will tell you this. It was not that I did not want Adam and Eve to know good from evil. I wanted him to rely on me and trust that I would give him all of the knowledge he needed to know. Really there was no evil that Adam and Eve were exposed to that they needed to know about at that time. I wanted to be the one to teach him the difference, not they themselves. Eating from that tree opened the doorway for Lucifer to have his way in the world, into the heart and mind of man. It tricked Adam into giving the serpent the gift I gave him, to have dominion and rulership, affecting the DNA of all generations to come. The fruit opened Adam and Eve's eyes, but what happened afterward when I came looking for Adam? He ran and hid himself because he was naked, as if that were an offense. But I never told him he was naked or that being naked was bad. You see, their perception had changed and they themselves became judges of what is good and what is evil, which was never supposed to be my creation's position. This changed our relationship, separating Adam, Eve, and I. A barrier was put between us, putting the creation at odds with the creator, because now they would not just obey me and trust me like before, but My Word would be constantly questioned. Each generation thereafter get a little more defiled, becoming judges of their own lives. My ways are truly not your ways, and with Lucifer's influence, man's ways have collectively gone astray more than once. You see the ramifications to this day where men are wise in their own eyes, twisting the bounds of righteousness with what they want to be good but in essence it is harnessed from pure evil that was unleashed by the fall."

"So why did you put the Tree there if you knew that they would potentially eat from it, with you knowing the ramifications of it?" Willow asked.

"Now that has a longer explanation and will take time for you to be able to comprehend. There is so much more I want to share with you, but you are not ready to hear, it would only confuse you. Trust me when I say it is all working out for good."

"I do trust you, Lord. I do," Willow said with confidence. Any doubt that she'd had before she walked into that room had vanished away. She made the conscious choice to never judge and question God ever again, realizing her own perspective was tainted.

"And one more thing. Never be afraid to ask me a question. This is what I desire. I want you to come to me as a child. Children are innocently inquisitive with endless desire to know truth. They are pure in heart, trying to figure out life and trusting that your answers are true. This is how you must be with me. You can ask me anything that you want, just as long as it is in humility and honesty without your own preconceived notions. Knock and I will answer. Understand?"

"Yes, I understand."

"Now, let's get down to business! I desire to send you back."

"Really? You mean give me back my life on Earth?"

"Yes, there is more left for you to do. Your time is not finished yet. I only hope that you see the value of your life now."

"Oh yes, I do, but to be honest I kind of want to stay with you. There is so much for me to learn here with you. I was not very good back there. I just couldn't get the hang of it."

"Do not worry, your home will be with me my child. But now I need you to go back. Your true purpose has yet to be fulfilled."

"What is my purpose?" Willow asked the question that she had wondered about for a very long time.

"Ahhh yes, the taunting question everyone wants to know. I assure you that when you go back it will be extremely apparent to you. But before I send you back, you must completely surrender and allow Me to reform you into a new creature. To do this you must come through the fire."

Willow thought for a minute because she didn't fully understand what the Lord was telling her. Then she looked at the burning bush and it became clear to her what she was to do next.

Willow took calculated steps towards the bush. She stood in front of it, a bit overwhelmed by the heat gleaming from the fire. She briefly thought about turning around and running right out the door, but quickly pushed that thought out of her mind. She was tired of running from God. She trusted Him, and maybe this process would hurt some, but for the first time in a long time she wanted His will to be done even if pain was involved. "How is this going to work?" Willow asked herself, evaluating the bush which came to her knees. The fire was not big enough for her to walk through. "Lord, this doesn't seem right. Did I understand you incorrectly? How am I supposed to do this?"

The flames flickered and the heat multiplied. "Don't be shaken by what you see and step out in faith."

"Ok, ok, ok Lord. I'm gonna do it. I'm gonna go on three." Willow tried to waste time. "ONE...TWO...THREE!" She lifted her leg to step over the bush but lost her nerve and put her foot back down. She put her hands on her hips, "I can't do it. I'm not ready!"

She grew tired of herself. *You are such a wimp, just do it,* she thought. "Ok, I got this. ONE..."

"WILLOW! I COMMAND YOU TO GO! NOW!" The Lord spoke and the fire turned a bright red with blue tips. Without thinking she took a dive over the bush into the fire and a portal swallowed her up.

Chapter Twenty

U pon her entrance the flames, projected higher into the air and the fire grew, dancing all around her with an unbearable heat. Just like the bush, the fire burned her but she was not consumed. It was like she had fallen into a big oven of flaring flames. She let out screams that came from the depths of her belly and stretched her vocal cords. Tears on her face quickly evaporated into fumes of steam. Her clothing melted off of her sweaty body. She felt a gripping pressure pulling on every part of her body and causing a black stream of a tar-like substance to ooze from her belly button. Then the malicious substance expelled from her ears and fingertips, and the fire raged on. Willow's screams turned to a loud roar. When she was about to holler again, it was interrupted by hard dry coughs, and then a glob of the substance came out of her mouth. Just when she thought she would lose consciousness, the purging was complete.

The flames quickly disappeared and Willow, being too weak tried to stand, stumbled backwards from exhaustion. She was saved right before hitting the floor by cool refreshing hands gently pushing her forward. A pearly white silk robe was glided over her head, concealing her bare body. Then she was picked up off of her feet and carried forward. Her eyes opened slightly, cautious of who had caught her. Holy Spirit smiled down at her and continued to walk forward. She exhaled, immediately comforted, falling asleep in the cool warmth of His presence.

"Wake up, Willow." Holy Spirit shook her shoulder. Willow weakly opened her eyes, rubbing them while looking around. Inspecting her surroundings, she noticed that she was in a new space. She sat up with a stir to fully assess the room. It was just as empty as the first one, but she noticed that she was up high on some sort of round platform high above the floor.

"Where am I?"

"You have gone through a lot, but you still have some to go in order to complete your transformation. The processing of the fire has softened you as clay and you are now on the Potter's wheel ready to be molded. You look so much better already!" Holy Spirit said as he knelt down beside her.

"I am glad that the fire part is over. A lot of nasty black stuff came out of me." Willow wiped her brow.

"You were purged and purified. Baptized in the fire, and your heart is fully restored. Now, you are clothed in righteousness."

She knew what He was saying was true, because she could feel the change that had taken place in her. She looked at her hands and they looked brand new. Her skin shimmered like golden glitter.

"Listen... when you go back it is not going to be easy. To tell you the truth, it will be much harder than before. Your spirit has been strengthened and elevated. So the things that you went through before are nothing compared to what you will have to face. You must be fully equipped when you go back, so I am going to go with you," Holy Spirit said, interjecting through her thoughts.

"I thought you would be there helping me anyway," Willow said still looking at her hands.

"Yes, but I be with you in a greater capacity. You will truly be a temple for me to dwell within. You'll be empowered by Me and walk in a greater measure of relationship with the Father."

"Okay. Yes, I think I need that as well. So what do I have to do for that to happen?"

"Remember these?" Holy Spirit picked up a basket from beside Him that held the fruit with different words engraved in them.

"Yes... I do!" Willow said with wide bugged eyes. Seeing the fruit made her remember how hungry she was.

"Here, take and eat and I will do the rest."

Willow grabbed the piece of fruit that said self-control. She took a big bite and juice ran down the side of her mouth. The sweetness delighted her and awakened more hunger within her. She ate quicker and quicker with each bite she took. Once one piece of fruit was gone, she moved to the next. As she ate, Holy Spirit slowly disintegrated into a strong wind and Willow was too focused on the fruit to notice what was happening. It was like once she tasted it she couldn't stop eating until all of the fruit in the basket was gone. Holy Spirit lifted her off the ground and spun her around in the wind. His presence fell upon her and just as she swallowed her last bite, an unfamiliar language poured out of her mouth.

Overwhelmed by the presence of God, she began to cry and her new heavenly language flowed out of her without constraint. She eventually stopped her worship and was gently laid back down onto the wheel in silence. She closed her eyes as the voice of the Lord spoke to her. "I, your Lord hath given you a new name. No longer will you wear the tag of the trees who weep. From now on you shall be called Lily, because I have given you beauty from ashes. Let this be a reminder to you that just as I take care of the lilies of the field, so will I always take care of you." Willow was overjoyed and fell asleep in the presence of the Lord.

LILY WOKE CONFUSED, with blurred vision. The room was so bright it took her eyes a few minutes to adjust and realize where she was. She heard a beeping sound and look over to her right and saw that she was hooked up to a heart monitor. To her surprise, she was in a hospital room. The door was opened, allowing chatter in the hallway to seep into the room. There were tubes connected all over her and her hand was sore from the IV that protruded from it. She pondered yanking it out, but decided that would probably cause a great deal of unnecessary pain.

Though dazed, she realized her mom was fast asleep beside her bed. Her mom had her hand gentle wrapped around Lily's other hand. She wondered how long she'd been gone and if all she had experienced was just an elaborate dream. Lily wiggled her hand from her mother's grip to rub her tired eyes, allowing her to get a good view of her wrist. The beeping of the monitor rapidly increased, correlating with the rate of her heartbeat. Around her wrist was the blackened scar, the imprint of the hand from the tortured being in the river of lava. Her suspicion had been put to rest. "It really happened," she whispered to herself.

DEATH STOOD IN THE doorway of the hospital room snarling as he watched Lily awaken from her lengthy sleep. Once Lucifer had found out that she would be revived, he had sent Death back on assignment to destroy her. After things didn't go his way in the garden, he sent the most insidious beings he could conjure to help in the matter - to finish her off.

Death walked into the room with a new army behind him. Divination, Python, and Heaviness creeped in, in a straight line one after the other. Death had new energy and was determined not to let his master down this time.

AFTER SOME TIME OF deep contemplation Lily calmed herself down and tried to sit up in the bed a little, but she failed due to being very weak. She struggled many times to push herself up, until finally she won the battle. She sighed loudly and took a deep breath from exhaustion. She held her head from dizziness, which had gripped her as soon as she sat up.

UPON ENTERING THE ROOM Divination, glided and stood beside Lily's bed, uttering incantations that were effectively weakening her. The demon's head of snakes hissed with every enchantment that was uttered. Death stood in a corner of the room, eagerly waiting for the spells to completely take root. Then Divination waved her bony hands with sharp nails towards Lily while gesturing with her head for Heaviness and Python to move forward with their attack.

Heaviness stood 10 feet tall, with a frame made of stone boulders eagerly waiting in the doorway. Once the signal was given from Divination, he ran toward Lily and with every step the room shook from the crushing weight. He jumped and bore down on Lily, swiftly pushing her back down on the bed. All the while, Divination continued to chant its sleeping spell draining her energy.

ALL OF A SUDDEN, A great invisible force threw Lily back down on the bed towards her pillow. Her eyes became heavy and hard to keep open, until they closed all the way as if she had gone back to sleep. The presence weighed down on her with supernatural strength. The hairs on her arms raised as she sensed the evil it carried.

SLITHERING BEHIND HEAVINESS, Python scurried across the floor with its insectoid legs, like a centipede. He crawled up on the bed, gliding up towards Lily's head, and slowly wrapped his body around her neck. He squeezed with all of his strength, sucking the life out of her with every exhale.

"You thought you would get away from me...HA! Nice try, but it's not gonna be that easy," the deep sultry voice of Death intensified as he walked with confidence towards the bed from across the room. "I have a message for you from my master. You can run but you can't hide. Ha Ha Haaa! It's time to collect."

Lily tried with all of her might to move and yell, but her body wouldn't budge and nothing came out of her mouth. She felt extremely drained as she struggled to breath. Fighting for every breath she eventually thought about giving up and letting the evil have its way. But a comforting yet stern whisper came from within, "Death and his helpers have touched you illegally, for though you walk in the flesh you do not war after flesh. Bind him in Jesus' name and pull down this defeated foe," Holy Spirit instructed.

Lily, still unable to move or speak, began to just think, *"Death and all of you unclean spirits, I bind you in the name of Jesus Christ and command you to flee, NOW!"* Immediately the presence lifted off of her.

Lily's eyes opened and she sprung forward in the bed, gasping for air while sweat dripped down her face.

HEAVINESS, PYTHON, and Death all flew back with great force away from the bed once Lily had commanded them with a thrust of powerful wind. Divination choked on its spells, and gasped for air while falling to the ground.

As the demonic spirits tried to regain their composure, Petundan and Michael walked into the room ready for battle.

LILY LOOKED ALL AROUND the room nervously as her heart was still beating out of her chest.

REALIZING THAT THE demonic forces were at a disadvantage, Michael leaped in the air with his sword drawn and landed before Divination, who was still knelt down on the floor. And with one clean stroke, he sliced its head clean off, causing the snakes to screech with pain until they quickly dried up to dust.

Heaviness came from behind Michael and wrapped his big arms around him and tried to squeeze, but Michael was too quick for him and he slid out of his grip, dropped to the floor and glided into a roundoff kick. The demon fell to the floor with a thud. Michael turned around to face his attacker and said, "You should quit while you're ahead." Heaviness jumped up swinging aimlessly in the air at Michael with no success of landing a punch, as Michael dodged every attempt. Then the demon grunted with frustration and got slower and slower with his strikes. "Get out of the way!" Death screamed as he grabbed Heaviness' arms and pulled them apart with rage, "You're no help! Let me show you how it's done!" Heaviness screamed and fell to the ground in a pool of dust.

Petundan stood by the door waiting for a chance to help Michael as Python quietly slithered his way. Once he got close enough, he aggressively wrapped his thick body around Petundan's legs causing him to fall to the ground, catching him off guard. Then he continued to wrap around him until Petundan's whole body was entangled and he was unable to move. He tried to release his wings but it was too late. The strength of Python's hold was too great. Petundan yelled in agony from the suffocation of Python's entrapping grip.

Michael was briefly distracted by Petundan's yell and was sucker punched in the gut by Death, which caused him to slide across the floor, hitting the wall. Death ran over and stood over him, roaring in laughter. "And you're supposed to be one of God's best. What a pity."

Meantime, Python hissed with his fangs out, glaring at Petundan's face, ready to take a lethal strike. Petundan closed his eyes and began to focus as he released some of his powerful light from within. The angel began to shine brighter and brighter blinding and paralyzing Python. Petundan's hopes of the demon getting releasing was quickly faded as its grip tightened from the paralyzing effect. On the other side of the room Death lifted his giant foot up over Michael, who's still on the floor, and prepared to stomp him in the gut. Michael who was temporarily dazed from the attack, was brought back to awareness when he saw Death's foot coming down upon him.

Before Death could make impact Michael rolled out of the way. He Jumped up with his sword in his hand. Death quickly turned to him and threw a punch. Michael dunked and pivoted as he swung his sword slicing through the top of demon's head shaped like a hammer. Death roared with anger and agony as black goo gushed down his face from the wound. He wiped the goo from his face as said, "Get over here!" Then he turned to Michael swinging, successfully connecting a punch to Michael's face. Michael stumbled but quickly regained his composure. Death lunged forward reaching out both of his hands to grab the angel in a tight grip. With Michael's renown speed, he leaped in the air, flipping over Death's head faultlessly landed behind him. Then he slashed his sword across the demon's back cutting him in two as more black goo splashed on the floor. Death pieces turn to dust on the ground. Michael performed a fancy swivel of his sword as he broke his combat stance, looking down at his defeated opponent.

Just then a blinding light appeared. "Ah! Well done, Well done my friend" the archangel Raphael said as he walked towards Michael. Michael dusted off his robe and picked up his shield that was lost in battle. "It's good to see you. But what are you doing here? Something must be wrong" Michael questioned with concern.

"Hey, hey... ahem, can I get a little help over here." A small, high-pitched voice said wheezing from the other side of the room. Petundan was still wrapped in the compressed squeeze of Python, who remained paralyzed. Michael and Raphael looked at it each other in shock. "Oh I'm sorry Petundan, I kind of forgot about you over there," Michael said holding back a chuckle.

"Oh wow Petundan, you really got yourself in a bind there, huh," Raphael joked.

"Please help," Petundan manage to force out of his crushed diaphragm.

Raphael swiftly spun his golden laser sharp boomerang towards Python sliced through each layer of his body that was wrapped around Petundan, releasing the angel. Then Raphael's weapon returned smoothly back into his open hand once its job was complete. "Huff! Petundan laid there loudly gasping for much needed air.

Micheal and Raphael walked over and helped Petundan up off the ground. "Thank you for your help," Michael said to Raphael.

"Yes, I had to rush here. The Lord has sent me to inform you that the time has almost arrived for the last battle," Raphael said.

"Then that means soon this war will finally be over," Petundan said with relief.

"Yes, that is true, my friend, but there is still so much to be done. Lucifer will surely intensify his works," Michael mentioned.

"I just hope she stays the course and truly grows upon what the Lord has given her. For this season will not be any easier than before," Petundan said as he turned to look back at Lily, who was still startled on the bed.

"WILLOW, YOU'RE AWAKE!" her mother yelled, awakened by her daughter's abrupt movement. Tammie stumbled to her feet, "Honey, are you okay?" she asked, concerned. Lily began to regain her composure, but was still weak from the struggle. Her mother pulled Lily's hair out of her face and caressed her cheek. "Something's wrong, isn't it? I'm going to get the nurse." She rushed to the door.

"No, mom, wait! I'm...I'm okay, come back please. Before you go get the nurse, I need to talk to you and it can't wait."

Tammie reluctantly turned around and went back to her daughter's side. Lily thought it fit that her mother would be the first person she would encounter coming back. She knew that God had set it up that way and she was happy about it.

Her mother sat on the bed beside Lily and held her in her arms and gently rocked back and forth. Lily rested her head on her shoulder. Tammie cried from the unexpected affection her daughter was showing her, which was out of her character.

"I thought we were going to lose you, but praise Jesus, He heard our prayers. He's not finished with you yet, honey. Your grandfather and brother were just here. Your grandfather was the one who found you and brought you here. We have all been here day and night with you. You know, you've been in a coma for about a month now." Lily raised her head to look her mother in the eyes. She couldn't believe she had been gone that long. "Uh huh.... but the Lord is faithful! He heard our prayers!"

"Mom, that is part of what I wanted to tell you. The whole time that it appeared that I was in a coma, I was with God. He has taught me many things and He's transformed me. He even gave me a new name! I'm not Willow anymore, Ma! He named me Lily because He said that He has given me beauty from ashes." Lily spoke with great excitement and grabbed her mother's hand. Tammie just looked at her with no expression on her face, trying to figure out what to make of it all. Was her daughter hallucinating or was she suffering from brain damage from all of the drugs she'd taken?

"Willow, honey, you were just dreaming, just wait here and I'll go get the nurse, okay."

"No mom, it wasn't a dream. Just listen to what I am saying and you will know that it is the truth. Listen with your heart and don't just hear the words that I am saying. I received the Holy Spirit and He baptized me; I'm changed. The Father, the Son, and the Holy Spirit have all taught me great things and have opened my eyes. I know that it's hard to believe, but I had a divine encounter with them. I am not the same and never will I be again. I have been given another chance, Momma!" Lily's eyes glistened as she spoke with such passion. Tammie had never heard her daughter talk in that way. It was like night and day.

She knew in her heart that her daughter was telling the truth. As Lily talked, she could see a physical change in the girl. She realized how much of her prayers the Lord had answered and she was thankful. Lily stopped talking for a moment and tightened her grasp on her mother's hand. She cleared her throat. "Momma, I am sorry for how I rejected you when you came back into my life. I was so filled with hate that I couldn't see the damage it was doing to us both. I forgive you for everything that has happened. I'm not the ultimate judge and so I am sorry for the ways that I in turn hurt you. I can't hold you hostage for things that happened in the past and for things you have no control over. I want us to have a real relationship." Lily smiled at her mother, who had an endless stream of tears flowing down her face. "I would absolutely love that, sweetheart." They grabbed each other and tightly embraced one another.

"Oh, there is so much I want to share with you!" Lily said.

"Me too; I have some awesome news to tell you! While you were in a coma, Louis woke up from his!"

Don't miss out!

Visit the website below and you can sign up to receive emails whenever Lakise Collins publishes a new book. There's no charge and no obligation.

https://books2read.com/r/B-A-JVTU-FSMAC

BOOKS 2 READ

Connecting independent readers to independent writers.

About the Author

Lakise Collins was born and raise in Charlotte NC and has always had a love for the creative aspects of life including music, art, and writing. She aspires to create content that will encourage the christian walk and utimately impact lives to draw closer to Christ.

Lakise can be contacted by email at: Lakise.Collins@gmail.com

www.ingramcontent.com/pod-product-compliance
Lightning Source LLC
Chambersburg PA
CBHW031203260626
47169CB00004B/1233